D1553221

# Where Love Finds You

Marilyn Grey

WINSLET PRESS

*Where Love Finds You*


To learn more about Marilyn Grey, visit her Web site:
www.marilyn-grey.com



Library of Congress Control Number: 2013940779

ISBN-10: 0985723505
ISBN-13: 978-0-9857235-0-7



Cover & Interior Design by Tekeme Studios

Printed in the United States of America

First Edition: May 2013
13 12 11 10 9 8 7 6 5 4 3 2 1

*To: 1224*

*For: Everything*

# Ch. 1 | Ella

Nine years ago, on a quaint corner of town, I met my husband and hadn't seen him since. Everyone said to move on, I'd never see him again, but I couldn't. If I did, I'd regret it for the rest of my life.

"Did you get that?" A tall, blue-eyed man said.

"I'm sorry. You would like a soy latte?" I glanced around. Every day I glanced around, hoping he would walk through the door and into my heart.

"Yes, please."

Another day, another normal day of life without him.

"There you go again," Dee, my dearest employee and most eccentric friend, said as she handed the man his latte. "Come on, Ella. Thinking about Mr. Right again, are we? I say this in love, but really, you have to realize that this is ridiculous."

I leaned against the counter and surveyed the happy couples in the coffee shop, some rings, some bare fingers, all smiles. "I'm getting older Dee. Nearing thirty. Being single isn't what I had in mind for my twenties, much less my thirties."

"Look at you." She waved her hand in front of me. "You own your own successful coffee shop without a college degree, you are beautiful inside and out, and you have accomplished more in life than most people I've ever met, regardless of age. You are quite the catch if you ask me, and do you know how many men walk through this door and give you that look? It's not like you have no options."

"I know." I doodled on the notepad in front of me. "All of this, the coffee shop, the stuff I do which really isn't as special as you seem to think, it's not something I take for granted at all. I know there are men who have been interested, but they aren't him. I have to wait for him as long as it takes."

"You, my friend, are about as idealistic as it gets. What if this guy is married now?"

"He can't be."

"You really believe in soul-mates, huh?"

"Not really. I just believe that he is the one for me and if he is married to someone else now, well, I can't get married to someone else until I know that for sure."

AFTER THE LAST HAPPY COUPLE LEFT *CHANCES*, MY LITTLE coffee shop, I cleaned up and turned the lights down. Another day over and a new one to look forward to. I locked the door and a blur of white, carried by the wind, landed near my feet. There, on the crumpled receipt, one person's treasure became someone else's trash. Just like it happened for me.

I picked up the receipt and looked for a phone number, but saw only memories. Soft, flowing strands of ink curled into my phone number. *My name is Ella. Call me sometime? 610-555-2949.* All those years I told myself he couldn't have found the receipt, someone else picked it up and threw it away, but sometimes I doubted myself and the years of waiting. I started to believe I was as crazy as everyone else thought. Perhaps he got the receipt, threw it in the trash himself, and laughed with his friends about girl number five-hundred and eighty who tried to become his girlfriend.

Eighteen. Only eighteen at the time.

I walked away from the shop and looked into the eyes of others as they passed me. So many people, so many chances to find love, why did I have to believe in only one person?

My phone rang.

I hit silent without pulling the phone from my purse, then sat on a bench overlooking a small park in the middle of the city. The trees caressed the air with their fingers, as I brushed my hair from my eyes and considered giving another man a chance.

"You'll grow out of it," Mom said.

"Once you hit thirty," Derek, my brother, said, "still single, you'll regret all of this nonsense,"

Only one person believed in me. My dear friend Sarah. Best friends since elementary school. We used to dress up and pretend to get married to our stuffed animals. She is the complete opposite of me in every way, but the one thing we always had in common is our love for love. We wanted to find love, stay in love, and evolve with love, and we'd wait forever to find the one person who would make that journey the best adventure it could possibly be.

WHEN I FINALLY WALKED UP THE STEPS TO MY APARTMENT A soft melody interrupted my typical thoughts. I followed the tune and saw an open window. Second floor, beautiful historic apartment building with white curtains blowing in the summer breeze. The piano melody matched the tempo of my life. Subdued, but dramatic. The curtains swayed with the song.

White draping fabric, like the dress I longed to wear. Yes, there were times I considered that years of waiting could eventually escort me down the aisle to a life of singleness.

I considered it. Many times.

The piano notes resonated with me again. Deeper, still soft and slow. I closed my eyes and imagined my violin in my arms, moving with me, with the piano across the street.

Back and forth, back and forth.

I stood up and opened the door to my apartment building. It's time, I thought. I need to consider moving on from the man I may never know.

# Ch. 2 | Matthew

My fingers always knew where to go on the piano. It's like they were connected to my heart when my mind couldn't wrap around what I felt. I'm not one of those guys. I don't sit around and process my thoughts all day long, analyzing every thing that goes in and out. Don't get me wrong, I analyze life around me, just not my own life. It's one of those things where I just don't want to know. Okay, who am I kidding? Maybe I do think a little too much, but there's something about the piano that helped me process my thoughts in a more peaceful way.

So, I'd sit down in front of those keys and let my fingers tell me what I didn't want to know. On that humid summer night, windows open, cross-breeze inspiring me to play, I sat down in the dining room of our apartment. In that little nook by the window, my piano waited for me, and every day I faithfully came and sat down for a little while. Today, I stared at the keys for a few minutes, then closed my eyes and let it come.

Sometimes I'd find lyrics, other times not. Tonight I couldn't find words, just knew I was lonely and tired of it.

"Matt," Gavin said from the other room. "What's with the depressing song, man?"

"It's where I'm at right now." My fingers continued to graze the keys, finding their place on the piano and my life. "Just where I'm at."

"Well, I hope it's not where you're going."

I laughed under my breath and switched the pace to *Lean on Me.* "Better?"

"Getting there. At least this song has a little hope somewhere in there." Gavin appeared beside the piano and sang with me.

We finished messing around and Gavin turned back into counselor. "Seriously, Matt, you really need to stop dwelling in your mind and live a little. You have so much going for you. Great life, great business, a beautiful girlfriend who wants to marry you tomorrow. What more could you ask for?"

"Yeah. It's just that all my ducks aren't in a neat line. They are running around in circles chasing their feathers."

He hit my back and walked away, then said from the bathroom, "Don't think about life more than you live it. Be content already."

"Content?" I entered the bathroom as Gavin swished some Crest around in his mouth. "You're thirty-one now. Let's say you find a girl tomorrow, get married in the next year, then start having kids in two years, you will be in your forties with young kids, and that's not counting some good old time with just you and the lady."

"Matt. Stop thinking so much and just live. You're missing out on right now because you're too busy thinking about tomorrow."

"Yeah." I walked away and stood in the hallway, looking around the bedroom I spent the last five years in. "It's just this empty bed."

Gavin jumped onto the flimsy mattress. "Hey, I'll sleep in here if you're lonely."

"Get up, man."

He blew me a kiss and huddled under the covers.

"Seriously. You always find a way to be annoying when I am the most annoyed at you being annoying."

"Isn't that the point?" Gavin's grin lit up the room. "Lighten up, Matt. Just lighten up, take a deep breath, and realize that everything will happen when it's meant to."

"Do you ever wonder 'what if?'"

"No, but I remember the last time you talked about it."

"You mean you never wonder about the past and think to yourself, 'What if? What if I could go back in time?'"

"It will all work out. Everything will work out."

"You say that even when everything is falling apart."

"Perspective. It's all perspective." Gavin entered the hallway and disappeared around the corner. "Hey, you can borrow my glasses if you want."

ANOTHER DAWN. ANOTHER DAY TO THINK ABOUT THE NEXT day. Gavin is right, I thought. I needed to calm down and live for once.

How could I be thinking like this before I even opened my eyes?

My sun rose later than most people. Owning my own business made life easy in that sense. I scheduled all of my jobs for late morning, early afternoon, because I'm pretty much as nocturnal as it gets and I like to sleep in a little.

Gavin likes to say I live two lives. One, as the guy who paints houses. And two, the guy who sits in his room all night and writes depressing songs for no one to hear but himself.

I guess that's true. Not that it's intentional or anything. I write songs because it helps me process what I'm going through, and, well, there is one other person who hears them.

Gavin's a good friend, really. We met at a homecoming dance when our dates ditched us and even worked at a local coffee shop together after high school. We don't have much in common, but that's what's great about our friendship. We really are brothers. I annoy him with my analytical thoughts about paper plates, and he annoys me with his joyful lightbulb that never goes out.

He is the balloon in my life and I'm the weight that keeps him from flying off into the clouds. And in other ways he is the same for me. Sometimes I thought I'd need to find a woman like Gavin since he's the only friend I've maintained for this many years, but at the same time, I've always wanted someone like me, someone to understand me like Gavin never will.

After a quick shower and a bowl of Raisin Bran, I left for work.

On the way, I passed that coffee shop again. The one I never go in. The one that took the place of the one Gavin and I used to work in. *Chances.* The new owner named it *Chances.*

I looked at the clock in my truck. Some extra time.

I pulled along the side of the road and checked out the interior of the shop. Eh, it's a long shot, but why not? Turning the car off, I exhaled and opened the door.

Why can't I just be normal?

The coffee shop looked nice. Better than what it looked like when I worked there. Course that owner cared about money and money only, so he did everything as cheap as possible.

The sweet smell of coffee woke me up a little more as I walked inside. Loved the photography and art on the walls. Reminded me a lot of Gavin's work, only not as unique. Gavin fuses reality with imagination. I stopped in front of a photograph of a brunette with long hair. Could only see the back of her, but I loved the way the sun hit her hair and shoulders, highlighting the beauty of a woman in such simplicity.

The sound of clinging spoons and the smell of coffee led me to the register.

"Can I help you?" A spunky tattooed girl said with a smile.

"Yeah, let me see. Anything you recommend?"

"Everything." Her smile widened. "You like iced or hot? Sweet or something a little different?"

"Hey, why not try something different today for once?"

"Alright, how about a surprise?"

"Sounds good. I could use a surprise right now."

"Okay, give me a few minutes."

I paid for my mystery drink and meandered about the shop again. Weird how many memories lived here. Felt like just yesterday.

I sat down and looked at the name of the shop, written in cursive on the window. Saw the place turn into *Chances* just a year ago, but it never interested me. I wanted it to stay the same. The change reminded me of the end of a road, a road I should've traveled years ago.

"Here you go, sir." The young girl tapped the counter and smiled at the paper cup that hid my liquid secret.

"Thank you." I picked up the iced mixture and took a sip. "Wow. Different is good. So what is it?"

"It's a Vietnamese blend. Really unique. Sour, sweet, salty all in one."

"Yeah. Wow. Definitely different."

Her laughed filled the quiet shop. "Glad you like."

A quick exchange of goodbyes and a few glances around the shop later, I walked back to my truck and thought maybe "the one" really didn't exist. Maybe I should've proposed to Lydia and moved on with life.

# Ch. 3 | Ella

A red truck pulled out from the parking spot in front of *Chances*. I pulled in behind it and jogged inside.

"Everything alright this morning?" I said to Dee.

"Just dandy. How about you?"

"Good. Sorry I'm late. I need the checks to deposit, then I need to make a quick run to the bank and Target. I'll be back after that."

She handed me the envelope of checks. "You know, it really is okay if you aren't here all the time. I can handle it, the other guys can handle it. It's okay to take a break sometimes."

"What's a break?"

"Really. Why not take the day off and go to a park or something? A museum? How will you ever meet someone if you stay in your coffee shop the rest of your life?"

"You know why I do this."

"Ella, go somewhere. Get out and do something. Just today."

"Maybe tomorrow. I'll be back in a few."

Dee worked there as much as I did, trying to save money for her own tattoo studio. I paid her well as my manager to help her out a little. I really love seeing people create their own businesses and do something they love.

She helped me out a lot, too. Went above and beyond. And even listened to my personal rants about life and love. I couldn't have asked for more.

"I KNOW, I KNOW." TOSSING MY PURSE ON THE COUNTER, I

smiled at Dee. "I really am starting to believe I'm crazy. I mean, I am pretty sure I've completely lost my mind at this point."

"You are just now tapping into reality, huh?"

She laughed as I exhaled and made myself a coffee.

The bells on the door interrupted my thoughts. I looked across the room and saw him. Just another *not him.* Another *not him* with a ring on his finger.

After he ordered his coffee and sat down by the window I whispered so only Dee could hear me. "Okay, I'm ready."

"Are you serious?"

"I think so."

"Okay, before you change your mind I will make this happen. But just so I know, what made you want to do this now?"

"I'm crazy, Dee. I've completely lost my mind. I'm going to be thirty soon. My one goal in life . . . well, the only one I really cared about . . . was to get married, have children, snuggle up to my love and watch a movie. I'm running out of life. What are the chances of meeting *the one*?"

"Well, according to you, the chances are slim, but worth the wait. Now you're saying it's not worth the wait?"

"He's never going to come, Dee." The bells rang again. A happy couple walked in the door. Hand-in-hand, holding my dreams. "He's never going to come."

"Alright." She wiggled her fingers and brightened the room with her quirky smile. "You can call me Cupid. I am going to find you a husband."

"Sounds . . . promising."

# Ch. 4 | Matthew

This time I sat down at the piano and refused to play the way I felt. Instead, I played the way I wanted to feel and hoped it would become reality. Upbeat and fun, my hands moved across the piano as I pulled words out of my future and sang along as they came to me. Before I knew it, my song melted into Elton John's *I Guess That's Why They Call it the Blues.*

The apartment door opened and closed. Footsteps complemented my song like quick taps on a snare drum. Gavin stood beside me, tapping his foot, singing along. "Laughing like children, living like lovers . . . ."

I stopped playing and stood up. Gavin walked into the living room and I followed. Black-and-white photographs, framed and matted, reminded me of life beyond the petty things I worried about.

"Is that new?" I said to Gavin, pointing at the color photograph hanging above the couch. "You done with the trendy umbrella woman now?"

"Yeah, it's new. Do you like it?"

I stood closer to the photograph and analyzed the grass. "It's just a picture of grass, man. What am I missing?"

"Look closer, but don't analyze too much. You know how it is with music. If you over-think the lyrics you get some strange meaning that never existed."

"Yeah, I get that, but all I see is grass."

"You're right. It's just grass." Gavin smiled. "And the picture of summer."

"Right." The light gray couch welcomed me. I put my hands behind my head and tapped my foot to the Elton John song still humming in my brain.

"I think you need to stick with painting pictures instead of snapping them with that camera."

"You're probably right, but I do like the color." He sat down on the chair across from me. "The black-and-white in here started to overwhelm me, especially with your depressing music every day. Besides, my friend is really good and we decided to teach each other. She's going to show me how to work the camera, and I'm going to show her how to use a paint brush to capture the same picture."

"What's going on with her? Sounds like you two spend a lot of time together. No romantic things happening as you hold her hand and show her how to paint those precious blades of grass?"

Gavin laughed and cracked his knuckles. Typical sign that he's uncomfortable, but doesn't want to show it.

"So, what is it? You like her or what?"

"I know it sounds crazy, but we're just friends."

"Just friends? Does that mean you like her, but she isn't interested?"

"You know my feelings on the subject. I'm not interested and she knows that. I don't think she's interested. Actually, if things don't work out with you and Lydia I thought of hooking you two up on a blind date."

"Nah, you know how I feel about those artsy types."

"What are you talking about, man? You're an artist. Musicians are artists too."

"Exactly. I can't deal with these types. Too emotional."

He smiled and walked away. Classic Gavin. He likes to have the last word, and it's always something sarcastic. One, two, three, cue the sarcasm.

Nothing.

"Whoa. No last words from Gavin today?"

"Too tired. I'm going to shower and watch a movie. You game?"

"Sure. I'll play a depressing song for you while you shower."

"You are a good friend. Always know how to keep joy in the house."

"Hey, welcome back."

DON'T KNOW WHAT IT IS, BUT EVERY TIME GAVIN WANTED TO watch *Braveheart* I know something's up. He isn't the type to talk about his feelings. I'm sure I do that enough for the both of us. Everything stays inside of him, like a deep well that occasionally shows its true colors when someone draws up some water.

That climactic speech of Mel Gibson's character. It always gets me too. Makes me want to go and do something. Something important. Which mainly turns into me writing another song for no one.

The credits rolled. Gavin closed his eyes.

I sunk my bucket into the well and gave a tug. "What's going on in the world of Gavin?"

Silence in the well tonight.

Another tug. "Hey, sometimes it helps to know you get depressed too."

He opened his eyes. "Not depressed."

"Then what? Just one word to describe the mystery that you are."

"Remember when you and Amber broke up?"

"That's not one word and that's got nothing to do with you."

"Right. I'm getting there."

"Okay, I remember. Of course. What about it?"

"Remember when she gave you the necklace back and you felt like you lost everything in that one action?"

"Why are we talking about Amber? High school romances can't be related to this time of our life."

"That night you called me. I still couldn't figure out what to do about college. Whether to stay or go."

"What does this have to do with anything?"

"Man, you have the patience of a four-year-old. I'm getting there."

I motioned for him to go on.

"That's the first time I ever heard you cry. Last time, too."

"Yeah. It wasn't a cry. I just choked up a little. Go on."

"Well, before that day I never thought much about love or marriage. I enjoyed single life. Maybe I just enjoyed attention, I don't know. But I thought about 'the one.' You know we always joked about it before, but then you got real serious about it after Amber. You were convinced that someone better, someone *right*, waited for you out there in the big sea of fish. Then you met Lydia, almost right away."

I nodded.

"Well, after that, I have been on a search for meaning in my life. Friends always ask me about art or music, saying I need to put my talent to work and get famous. You know, before you called me that day I believed that fame would be the best road in my life."

"So how did my breakup change your life?"

"It didn't." He stood and stretched his back. "It just made me realize that I wanted a woman and I'd sacrifice anything in my life to find her."

"Okay . . . ."

"What?"

"I didn't understand the grass in the picture above my head, and I can say that I really don't see where you're going here either."

He laughed. "Everything has to have some kind of logical point to you, doesn't it?"

I GUESS THAT'S WHY THEY CALL IT THE BLUES. ALL THIS TIME on my hands, painting endless houses for endless married couples, could have been time spent with my wife. Gavin waited for her. Sacrificed for her. Whatever that meant. And he did it with joy. How is that even possible? I can understand those guys who like to look at everything on the menu and keep going back to the buffet for something new, but guys like us who actually want a nice woman to settle down with?

See, here's where my analytical nature ties me up and beats me to death. So many people around me, mostly other men, but hey, some of my women friends get pretty cynical too. They believe that life is filled with a bunch of choices and we just have to pick good, better, or best. No one person perfect for us. Just good, better, or best. We can settle for good, or we can wait around hoping for best and end up single until we're fifty.

I'm not convinced.

Now, I'm sure life is filled with choices. There's no doubt about it. Choices are one thing, though. And in my humble opinion . . . every choice I make will lead me to the one, the only one, at the right time. The only problem is I can't figure out how to know for sure when I've found the one. Did I already?

It crushed me when Amber gave me that necklace back. Twenty-four years old with the world at my fingertips. I thought I had it all. Beautiful girl, high school sweetheart, great life. And it all crumbled to the ground when her feet turned that city corner one last time.

I did. I'll admit it. I believed she was the one. Now, I know better. It would've never worked. She liked attention, I liked to sit on the sidelines. She liked to smoke cigarettes, I liked to throw them in the trash. This is where my cynical friends get me. They say we create the one out of whoever we happen to fall in love with.

See, life is full of choices. Tons of them. Every day I wake up. I choose what time to wake up and start my day. Then, I choose whether to stop and get a donut or go straight to work. Everywhere, all the time, I choose. Constantly.

And I believe, honestly, that all of these choices make a difference. One day, my choices would lead me to an altar, where'd I'd stand as my bride smiled at me from the big wooden doors.

Some people respond, "What if you make the wrong choices?"

And this is where I stop. I don't know. I don't know if I'm crazy. I don't know if the vast majority of people settling for good are right.

But, at least for now, I still believed in one. Just one.

# Ch. 5 | Ella

Nothing like the smell of freshly cut grass with the gentle sound of a humming air conditioner. My friend Tylissa's husband stepped outside to cut the grass and we stayed inside, admiring her growing belly. Her living room matched the light mocha of her skin. Somehow refreshing and warm all at once.

"Still living in the city?" She said, hand atop her little person.

"Yeah. For now. Sarah and I live well together and I've gotta stay within walking distance to the shop."

"How's the business going?"

"It's great. I make more than enough for one person."

She glanced down at her swollen abdomen. "I'm sorry, Ella."

"No, no. Don't be sorry. That life inside of you is a beautiful thing. I'm not jealous, I promise you. It will all happen for me when it's right."

"Speaking of which, when is it right? Are you dating anyone?"

"You know how I feel about dating just anyone."

"I know, I know, but I can see it in your eyes. I know you want this." She looked around the room.

Somehow that one motion conveyed everything she wanted it to. Wedding pictures around the room, trailing up the steps to the room prepared for a new baby to discover its life. No longer *his* and *her* furniture, but *ours*.

"You're right," I said. "I do want this, but not with the wrong person."

"What about the guy you met a few weeks ago?"

"His name is Fred. I can't marry a Fred."

"He was nice looking, seemed friendly, and you don't want to give him a chance because his name is Fred? You think I liked my husband's name right away? I couldn't even spell or pronounce it for the first few months."

"You grew to love it. Mwenye is not that bad. Fred? No way. I can't grow to love Fred."

"Come on, girl. Are you for real?"

The back door opened.

"Hey love, come here a second."

Mwenye entered the room. Ragged jeans and ripped t-shirt hugging him. He smiled so bright you couldn't help but feel a sense of peace.

"Hello again, Ella." He wiped the sweat from his forehead, right above his scar.

"Hey, how are you? It's been a while since I've been here. I love what you guys are doing to the place."

"Thank you, thank you." He turned to his wife. "Everything okay?"

"Could you do me a favor, please?"

"Sure, what is it?"

"A glass of water would be nice."

He smiled, bowed his head to me, and trailed off into the kitchen.

"That's a good man you have there."

"He really is. I bet Fred is just as nice."

Over the next half-hour of our visit, Tylissa and I sipped ice waters made with love by Mwenye, as she practically forced me to write down a list of everything I wanted in a husband.

"Okay, let me see it," she said after I wrote the forty-second quality.

"This is embarrassing."

"Oh, come on. Just let me see it."

I handed her the paper. She took it, folded it up without reading it, and ripped it into shreds. One piece after another fell into her lap.

"A list," she said with a smile, "is silly. No one can measure up to a list, not even you. So, let's move on with life and give the Fred's in the world a chance."

She had a point.

AFTER ANOTHER HALF-HOUR WITH TYLISSA I SAID GOODBYE to the family of three and went back to the coffee shop.

"You are kidding me," Dee said when I walked through the door.

"I guess I have nothing else to do. I'm trying, I really am."

"You're trying? Visiting a friend you haven't seen in months for an hour isn't my idea of trying." She walked to me, grabbed my shoulders, and spun me around. "Go. You need to go. I will take care of it. Everything is fine. You pay me well for a reason. Why are you so afraid of being away from the shop?"

I looked away from her gaze. Her eyes could've burned a hole right through my mask if I gave her enough time to stare me down. One bad choice, one moment in my life of not being prepared, and look what happened. All of my dreams. Lost. Just like that. I didn't want to miss anymore chances.

"Go. Really. It will be fine." She pushed me out the door and walked away.

I walked to the corner of the street, hands in the pockets of my dress, and stood on a corner with four choices. For a few seconds I looked around, then started walking without a destination, without thought. Dee hadn't the slightest clue. One choice cost me so much. One choice. That's it. If I would've done things differently that day. Gotten ready quicker. Not given that handsome guy in our apartment building the time of day. So many things would be different. I made every bad choice I could possibly make in one day, on that very day. And my life hasn't been the same since.

The hustle and bustle of rush-hour in Philadelphia. So many cars, so many people. All going about their normal day. I looked up to the sun-lit sky. Not one fluffy cotton ball hanging in the blue expanse. How often do I stop and look up? I wondered. Every day, I ran around doing whatever I could, waiting for love to find me, never taking time to look up and remember that life is bigger than me and dreams of romance. Maybe love would never find me. Maybe I needed to find it.

"Look at you," Sarah said, camera in her hands. "Walking around the city in the middle of the day?"

"Yeah," I smiled. "Hell does feel a little on the chilly side today, huh?"

"Chilly? It's turned into an ice block. What are you doing?"

"Living."

"Sounds nice. Maybe I can snap a few pictures of you then. Your first day back to life." She smiled and fiddled with her camera. "I just finished snapping some pictures of a few friends of mine. Some engagement photos, some just for fun. I thought of you."

"Why me?"

"Oh, just a certain friend of mine."

I could've been standing in the middle of the street and wouldn't have realized it. "What?"

"I took some shots of him today. I have them here in the camera."

"For a second I thought you were talking about him."

"It's probably not him. Here." She clicked around and handed me the camera.

"Well, this could be my answer."

The happy, gorgeous man taunted me.

"Well?"

My eyes welled with tears, not enough to fall, just enough to show me I still believed. "It's not him."

"What do you think though? Worth a chance?"

I shook my head. We walked to another intersection. I followed Sarah's lead.

"So," she said. "I'm going to take some pictures of you in a graveyard."

I laughed. "How charming."

"I have an idea. You'll see."

We crossed another street and people crossed our paths. One after another. Where were they going? What were they doing?

"So," Sarah said. "If you happen to find this man of your dreams, who you don't even know anything about, do you really think you'll fall in love and live happily ever after?"

"Not at all." I continued to follow her lead. She walked so much faster than I did. Out of breath, I continued, "I don't expect him to be perfect, and I don't expect our marriage to be perfect either. We'll have our flaws and our marriage will be flawed, but I just know he's the person I want to have flaws with."

"Interesting enough."

"How do I explain this?" A few cars blurred by as we waited to cross another street. "It's like this . . . I don't believe that happily ever after means we never have disagreements or go through conflicts. What I do believe is that there is someone who is willing to stick through all of these things with me, because we love each other more than we love ourselves."

"And you don't believe that can happen with any number of men in the world? Just one? And you haven't even met this guy. How do you know for sure he is everything you think he is?"

"Honestly, that's something I don't know the answer to anymore. All I know is I saw this guy when I was still a girl in this world, and after all of these years, I can't get him out of my head. It's like his picture is glued to the back of my eyelids and every time I wake up, he's there. Every time I go to sleep, he's there. I've tried to replace his picture with someone else. Believe me, I've tried, but it always shows up again. It sounds romantic, but it's starting to feel like a nightmare."

MOST OF MY FRIENDS WERE MARRIED. AND MOST OF MY married friends had children. I can't tell you how thankful I was to share an apartment with Sarah. She didn't spend her twenties partying. She hated bars and cigarettes. Always kept the house clean and never got upset at me for leaving my shoes in random places. More than anything, though, she didn't have a husband. That sounds terrible, doesn't it?

I always wanted the best for my Sarah. I really did. If she got married and asked me to be the maid-of-honor I would have jumped at the honor. It wasn't jealousy. It was the fact that one person in my life, the one closest to me, understood the empty feeling of curling up under the sheets and not having a man's body to drape your legs over top.

Loneliness didn't consume Sarah, though. She truly enjoyed every second of her life. We spent the next weekend cleaning our apartment together before our trip to Cape May, New Jersey. End of the summer getaway. Something I hadn't done in years.

As she wiped down the kitchen counters on a sunny Saturday morning, she hummed a cheery melody.

"How can you always be so happy?" I said.

"If I tell you my secret, will you keep it confidential?" She tossed a paper towel in the trash can. "A spoonful of sugar helps the medicine go down."

"I think I can keep it between us." I finished putting the last of the dishes into the white cabinets. "You'll have to let me know what kind of sugar you use though."

"Honestly, I have my days. My bad days probably look like your average days though. There's no secret really. I think to myself . . . I could die any second. Right now, I could have cancer eating away my life. I could get in the car today and be gone, just like that."

"So, thinking about death makes you live life with more joy?"

She laughed. "You could look at it that way. Thinking about death makes me want to live more. It makes me appreciate every second more. And in all of those seconds I'm given, I want to love. To give myself to others constantly."

"Serving others? Is that what brings you joy?"

"No, my friend. It's my joy that makes me want to serve others more. But it's not just about that. It's about giving something back. One day we're all going to be dead. What kind of memory will I leave behind in the hearts of those who knew me? A black cloud or a sunny day?"

"Definitely a sunny day." I looked at my left hand and the missing ring on that special finger. "I'm afraid I am the black cloud, huh?"

"Not at all. You are a hurricane. You've got wind, hail, crazy disastrous weather, but there in the center you have peace and sunshine."

"I think I'd rather be a black cloud."

She laughed. "You are unpredictable. Sometimes you are predictable because you want to be, other times you switch it up. I don't know what to expect with you, only to expect the unexpected."

"I guess I am kind of like a hurricane. What kind of man would want to marry a hurricane? You'd think two black clouds could find love together, but no one wants to run full-force into a hurricane."

We finished cleaning the kitchen in silence. My brain sifted through memories, wondering who would show up at my funeral and what they would say. She's right. What kind of impact would I leave? What imprint would I stamp on the history of this world?

The kitchen sparkled from top to bottom as Sarah and I walked into the living room.

"I think we've got everything cleaned now." She looked around the room. "And I've got everything packed. What about you?"

I picked up my planner off the crisp white coffee table, opened it, scanned my checklist, then said with confidence, "Yes."

"You want to know my first spoonful of sugar for you?"

"Huh?"

She took my planner and ripped a few pages out.

"What are you doing?" I reached for it. "Are you crazy?"

She pulled back, laughing. "I am known to be crazy."

"Seriously, Sarah. I love that thing."

"This thing"—another rip—"does not love you."

Knowing I would not win, I sat on the couch. "I don't understand what my planner has to do with anything. Why can't everyone just let me be? Everyone is always trying to fix my life. Ripping up planners, forcing me on car trips away from the shop, none of this is going to make me find a husband."

"Okay, rule number one. No planning. Just live, okay? I miss the old Ella." She sat down next to me. "Rule number two. Stop relating every instance in your life to your future husband, if you even have one. For all you know, you could end up single for the rest of your life."

I looked around at our bags. "Are you ready to go now?"

"Don't be mad at me." She held my hand. "I'm not trying to fix you. Trust me, that's beyond my capabilities." Her laugh never hid from life. Always there. Even in the most unwanted times. Like now.

"Seriously, Ella. I'm trying to love you. To get you out of this mood you have been consumed by and help you find some laughter again."

"Okay, okay. Are you ready to go?"

We picked up our bags and walked into the hallway. She locked the door, I walked down the steps and out the front door of our apartment building. Together, we stepped outside and inhaled the scent of a humid city morning. Cars swished by, creating blurs of color and bursts of different music. The bright green leaves glistened in the morning rays.

"Do you hear that?" Sarah said as we walked to her car.

"It's someone in that building." I pointed to the left at the beautiful, historic hotel-looking building. Similar to the one we lived in. "I think we can see their window from our apartment. I've tried to look, but couldn't see much. Whoever it is plays amazingly on the piano."

"Wow. I love that."

We piled our stuff into her car and hopped aboard the Nissan Altima. She turned up the music. I pressed the button and watched my window disappear into the car door. I could still hear the piano as we drove off.

Sarah never asked, but I knew she was thinking it.

# Ch. 6 | Matthew

Lydia came over Saturday morning. I opened my apartment door to see her emerald eyes staring into mine. She smiled, that weak smile that wanted more from me than I could give. I tried to smile back, took her hand, and pulled her into the apartment. She took my other hand, squeezed, and closed her eyes.

"Play me a song." She walked into the dining room.

I followed. Watched her hips move with her graceful walk. Her strawberry-blonde hair sweeping over her shoulders and climbing down her back. She placed her hand on the keys, turned her face just so. Bands of sunlight sparkled in her eyes from the open window in front of her. In the secrecy of my mind I touched her cheek and pushed the hair out of her face, behind her ear, like I did so many times before.

She looked down, waiting for me to play something.

"Are you sure?" I said and took a step closer to the piano.

She nodded and stepped aside. I took my place and set my fingers on top of the keys. I closed my eyes, inhaled, exhaled, and began to play. Minutes traced the silence of our relationship, drawing a picture of unanswered questions. My song echoed the unknown. The very thing she didn't want to hear.

As I played the last note she sighed. "I guess I have my answer."

I took her hand in mine and looked up at her closed eyes. I hated that I made her cry.

"I love you," I said.

"I don't see your love, Matthew." The only person who still called me Matthew after knowing me for years.

"It's just not the right time."

"I can't wait anymore. I can, but I'm not willing. I want a family, a husband who loves me. I'm tired of waiting for you to figure out with your mind what your heart already knows."

"I just need to figure things out."

"What's there to figure out?" She readjusted the bag on her arm and walked into the living room.

I trailed behind her, watching her hair glow, wanting to hold her again.

"There's nothing to think about," she said. "If you don't know that I'm the one you want to be with for the rest of your life at this point, then how will you ever know? It's not like we just met. I know everything about you, Matthew. You know everything about me. If you don't know by now, you will never know." She opened the door. Her eyes, that soft glow still there, like I had never hurt her at all.

How could she still love me?

"Do you hear me?" One foot outside of my apartment, the other inside.

I didn't want to hear her.

"Why don't you talk to me?" Both feet outside of my apartment. "This is all I can take. I love you." One tear landed on my bare foot. "I will always love you."

And with one last touch of my arm, she left.

STAMPED IN MY MEMORY. THE FIRST TIME LYDIA WALKED into my life. Her long, wild hair curved around her face and clung to her cheeks. My brother sat on the couch waiting for her. I sat in the dining room working on a college Psych paper. She looked in my direction and sat next to Andrew. His face beamed, so did mine.

She held his hand. "Andrew, how are you today?"

No response. Only a smile as big as Pennsylvania.

"I brought some puzzles." She pulled out a few toys and a puzzle.

He rocked back and forth, smile stretching to Ohio.

She looked at me again. I looked away, pretending to type on my laptop. Fingers flying a mile a minute, typing nothing and looking at her smile every chance I could. I watched her talk with my brother, one of the only other people besides myself who could make him smile like that. A bright joy in her presence hugged anyone who came within ten feet of her. My brother loved her immediately. I couldn't blame him.

She took him down to the basement to play and Mom wasted no time. "Pretty, isn't she?"

I nodded.

"Nice, too."

I nodded.

"She smiled at you."

My grin walked its way to Indiana.

"And you're still smiling."

I closed my laptop and looked at the light coming from the basement, then ripped a sheet of paper out of my spiral notebook and scribbled a note. I looked around the room, then saw her purse on the couch. Very trusting of her. I slipped the note into her bag and went to my room. A few minutes later she came up from the basement.

"Thank you for sharing your son with me, Mrs. Ryan. He is wonderful."

"Which one?" Mom laughed.

I wish I could've seen her face. "I will be back next Wednesday."

"That sounds great, Lydia. You have a safe drive home now."

The door closed. I hurried to the window in my room. She opened her car door, sat down, and smiled that beautiful smile of hers. She must've reached for her keys and saw the note, because she stopped to read something. I backed away from the curtain and peeked through a small slit. She looked toward our house and gave a thumbs up.

She couldn't have seen me. Could she?

I played some music and waited the rest of the night for her to call.

LYDIA ALWAYS LOVED ME. THERE'S NO DOUBT ABOUT IT. FROM that first thumbs up to the last chance she gave me as she stood by the piano, waiting for me to serenade her with our future as husband and wife. Only I played a depressing song. Again.

Gavin stumbled out of his bedroom and found me in the living room, still holding the door knob.

"What's going on?" He scratched his head. Eyes still adjusting to the summer light. "Thought I heard you playing something depressing again. Could've been a nightmare though."

"Good morning to you too."

"Thought I heard Lydia."

I nodded and closed the door.

"She really letting you go this time or what?"

"I hope not."

"Come on, man. You can't string the girl along forever. You know how lucky you are to have a love like that. And you want to throw it all away for some stupid reasons that make sense to no one but yourself."

"I don't want to string her along. Maybe if she finds someone better then I'll know it wasn't meant to be."

"What you're looking for doesn't exist, Matt."

"Then what are you waiting for? You are looking for the same thing."

"No." He pointed to my chest. "I'm looking for what you already have."

"This goes down as a great moment in history."

"What does?"

"The first time Gavin Kessler was jealous of something I had."

"Not jealous. Don't get ahead of yourself. I will have my girl soon."

"Don't be so sure of yourself."

"So what's your plan for today?"

"Need to run a few errands, give an estimate to someone, then nothing." I walked to the kitchen and poured a glass of orange juice. "What about you?"

He followed and poured a glass for himself. "No plans here."

"Shocking."

We downed a glass and poured another. "Was thinking of taking a drive to the beach."

"A drive to the beach? Why?"

"Who needs a reason to drive to the beach?"

"Long drive for no reason."

"Want to come?"

"No, thanks."

"Come on."

"Nope." I set my empty pulp-covered glass into the sink. "Hey, I tried *Chances* the other day. It's pretty nice in there. You'd probably like it."

"Oh yeah, I have a few friends who have their art in there. I should talk to the owner and see if I can get some of my paintings on the wall. Another guy I know sold some of his work for $3,000 a piece."

"No question there. I'd definitely ask."

"Yeah, maybe I'll head in there now. You wanna come with me?"

I looked at my watch. "I don't know."

"Run errands later." He tapped my watch. "Come with me."

A few minutes later we were walking down Spruce Street in the 80-degree humid morning. Without Gavin I'd probably had spent most of my twenties alone in my apartment watching too much Jack Black and Adam Sandler.

We rounded the corner onto South 15 Street, walked a little further, and came up to *Chances* on the corner of South 15 and Latimer. I opened the door and Gavin walked in.

"What a gentleman." He laughed and scooted in the door.

We walked up to the woman at the register, same as before.

"Nice to see you again," she said. "And I see you brought a friend."

"Hey, actually I was wondering if I could talk to the manager," Gavin said. "Is he around?"

"Actually, that would be me. What can I help you with?" She piled a mountain of whipped cream on an iced coffee and placed it on the counter. "Kenny, your drink is up."

A slender man took the coffee, tipped his hat, and said, "Thanks, Dee. Be back tomorrow."

"Rise and shine. See you then." She looked back to Gavin. "So, what was it you needed?"

He eyed the photographs on the wall. "Actually, I'm wondering if I could show you some of my art. Maybe sell a few of them here in the coffee shop."

"Oh, oh. That's not my area. You will need to talk to the owner about all that."

"Okay. Thank you," he said. "Is he here?"

"She"—Dee laughed—"is away for the weekend." She looked up at the chalkboard menu behind her. "Anything you guys want?"

"Surprise me," I said. "With something different than last time, too."

"Wow, Matt." Gavin leaned onto the counter. "This is quite the unusual happenstance."

"I'm spreading my wings."

Dee laughed, so did we.

"I'll take an iced white mocha latte with some caramel in there for good measure," Gavin said.

"Coming right up. Oh, wait." She pressed a few buttons on the register. "Total is 9.82."

I pulled out my wallet.

Gavin pulled out his. "I got it, Matt."

"You paid for pizza last week. I'll get this."

He put his wallet back in his pocket and scanned the walls. He stopped at the same picture that caught my eye last time. I knew he would. Hands in his pockets, he kept walking and stopped at a black-and-white picture of a woman's silhouette. Violin at her side.

"I've seen this before," he said.

"Really?" The girl said from behind the counter. "That's the owner actually. She used to play the violin."

I took the surprise drink she handed me. "Used to?"

"Yeah. She's never told me why she stopped. I never asked either."

I took a sip of the drink and looked at Gavin, deep in thought. "Where'd you see it before?"

"I don't know," he said. "Somewhere." He walked back to us and took his drink. "I had a friend who sold some art in here. Paintings. Do you guys still take that kind of thing? Or just the photography?"

"Anything." The girl rubbed her wrist where she had a tattoo of a bracelet. "She loves all kinds of art. You can submit music too if you're into that. You can even play a show here if you want. She's pretty picky though."

Gavin thanked her for her time, said he'd be back in a few days to drop some things off and talk to the owner. We walked out together.

"You should play a show there," Gavin said to me. "Some nice moody piano. Can't go wrong there."

"Love you too, man."

"She's a brick and I'm drowning slowly." Gavin sang the rest of the way home. A smile painted under his eyes the entire time.

I tuned him out. Pictured Lydia's sun-shiney face on the other end of the phone. The night she finally called me. She waited until Friday. I'm not one for those three day rules. Why wait if you like the person? It's annoying.

She waited two days. Not as bad as three, I guess. I didn't recognize the number on my cell phone and figured I'd probably hear her voice on the other end. When I did, a smile lit my face from that moment until the next time I saw her. They say it takes more muscles to frown than to smile. Could've fooled me. Every time I got off the phone with her I had to rub my jaw for three hours.

That's about how long we talked, too. At least the first night. The second night we talked until four in the morning. I can't remember what we talked about. She can't either. All we remember is laughter. And her sweet voice. I still love her voice. Especially when she sings to me.

All those times we'd sit at the piano. I'd play and she'd sing with me. Somehow we never made it through a song without our lips touching.

Maybe I couldn't imagine my life without her.

Gavin opened the door to our apartment building. "What are you thinking about?"

"Guess."

"If you love her, then marry her. What's so hard about that?"

We walked up the stairs to our apartment. I unlocked the door and walked inside, Gavin following behind me.

"I don't know," I said, flopping my keys on the end table by the door. "We have tons of good memories. I miss her every time we break up, but I wonder if I miss her because there's no one else. I miss the idea of her. The idea of having a girlfriend. But not her. She deserves for me to miss her."

"You mean you don't miss her at all? You just miss having a girlfriend?"

"I guess." I walked into the dining room and imagined her sitting at my piano the first day Gavin and I moved in. "Sometimes I think I miss her because we've been together since we were so young, right after my high school romance came to a crashing halt. There isn't an important memory in my life from then to now that doesn't include Lydia."

"And you're saying you want to start over with someone new? Find something better?"

"No." I sat down at the piano. "There is no one better than her. Just different. Someone different. Something new, exciting. You know, Lydia and I have spent our twenties together, growing into adults together. We were off and on for so many years. We had so many down moments. Maybe I want to fall in love with a woman, instead of a girl. Maybe I want to know what it feels like to be with someone else."

"That's not really fair to her."

"I know." I pressed down on a low A key. "That's why I need to let her go."

# Ch. 7 | Ella

The bridge from Philadelphia to New Jersey is so beautiful. Something about it inspires me every time I cross it. Except this time Sarah's iPod just so happened to play a familiar tune, one that made me sink down into the seat and ignore the gorgeous landscape.

"What's wrong?" Sarah turned the music down.

I looked out the window, ignoring her question.

"Oh. I'm sorry, Ella. I didn't realize my iPod was on still."

Silence carried us to the other side of the bridge. Over the same river I got stuck on the night I lost my dreams.

"That was weird timing," she said, looking for my reaction.

My gaze didn't leave the window.

"How long are you going to let this eat at you?"

"Easy for you to say," I snapped. "You still have your camera in your hands."

"I'm sorry."

I exhaled and looked at her. "I'm sorry. Didn't mean to react like that. It's just that you still take pictures, just like you did when you were a kid. There's only one thing I've wanted to do since I was a kid and it's been taken from me, all because of my stupid choices back then. If only I would have—"

"There are no 'if only's' in this life, Ella. You know, you wouldn't have met this man you are waiting for if it weren't for your choices back then. That night may have scarred you forever, but it also gave you him . . . something to live for. And you have been living for mysterious Mr. Right for the last few years. You don't need to zero in on one thing like this to find joy.

You can be happy no matter what your circumstances are. You don't need dreams and fantasies to be in love with life. Just live your life and you will fall in love with everything around you."

I avoided her gaze.

"I love you. I hope you know that. And loving you means telling you the truth. Trust me, it kills me that you feel that way, but photography isn't my dream. It never was. Sure, I love it and it's fun. I love that I get to make a living off of my favorite thing to do and I don't take that for granted. But it's not my dream."

I finally looked into her gentle eyes. She did love me. I knew she said these things out of love.

"My dream is every day. When I wake up, I want to find something new. Something beautiful about each day I'm given. I want to take the cards I'm given and play them with a smile, not to win, just to play. My hands could be sliced off and I wouldn't spend my life trying to find a way to snap pictures with my feet. I would pick up the cards I'm given and enjoy the game. That's my dream. To live today. Tomorrow may never come."

"Not according to Annie. She thinks the sun will come out tomorrow, clearing away the cobwebs and the sorrow."

"Annie needed hope. We all need hope. Maybe she was just looking in the wrong place. Hope doesn't need to come tomorrow, it can come right now. We don't need perfect circumstances to find hope. Annie didn't need caring parents to find hope. Hope lived in her, she was just too focused on her surroundings to realize it."

"You have gotten much more introspective over the last few years."

"I guess that's what being single does for a person. Too much time to think."

"Cheers to that."

WE ARRIVED IN CAPE MAY, CHECKED INTO OUR BED AND breakfast by the beach, and immediately walked out to the shore. Sarah, of course, brought her camera. Honestly, the thing seemed to be permanently attached to her hands. Not so good for me, because I spent more time with her than anyone else. If she didn't ask me to pose as a subject, well, then she'd ask me to hold up a reflector or a flash or something to help.

I always wanted to be a photographer, but it just didn't work for me. A few times Sarah let me borrow her back-up camera. I'd meander about the city, take a few pictures here and there, and come back with nothing exciting. Music came natural to me, the other areas of art . . . not nearly as much.

I guess that's why it was so difficult for me to see others blossoming in their own creative expressions. I would probably never be able to play the violin again.

"What are you thinking?" Sarah asked as her camera collected images of the frothy shores.

"Just wonder how different things would be if I didn't miss that flight."

"Yeah." She rolled her finger over the tiny button on her camera. "But if you keep trying to fix the past and plan your future you will never live today."

"Fortune cookie quote?"

We laughed.

Sarah sat down and pushed her toes under the sand. I did the same.

"There's something beautiful about the beach," she said. "Something so peaceful."

"So, what's on your mind lately? Anything deep and interesting?"

"Not really." Another wave crashed against the shore. "I did meet a guy though. I haven't wanted to tell you. Didn't want to upset you."

"Why would it upset me? I want you to be happy. Just because I'm spending my life waiting around for him to come back into my life, well, that doesn't mean I don't want you to get married."

She smoothed her wavy blonde hair behind her ear. "I know."

NINE YEARS AGO. HOW CAN NINE YEARS FEEL LIKE JUST YESterday and decades ago at the same time? I walked into the coffee shop that stood in the very place *Chances* now resides, his eyes immediately caught my attention.

Bright eyes, charming smile, hat tilted just so. A few co-workers stood beside him, laughing and talking. I can't even remember what they looked like. Whenever I found the courage to look up, my gaze fixed itself on him.

And him only.

Sadly, my friend Kate ordered our coffees before I arrived, so I had no real excuse to go to the register and talk to him. She even ordered a dessert for our late-night girl time. Again, no excuse to talk to him.

Kate and I talked for a while. She talked mostly, then said, "Ella, are you with me tonight? What's going on?"

I didn't want to say. Kate had broken up with her long-term first love. They met in middle school and became best friends, started dating in ninth grade, went through everything together during all four years of high school, then broke up when he went away to college and found someone else. Last thing I wanted to talk about was the guy looking at me across the coffee shop.

"I'm here. You are enjoying being single now?"

"Yeah, I think so. I feel free in a sense. My options are open. I'm not tied down. I want to enjoy the next few years and see where it takes me."

"I understand completely. I'm glad you've found freedom and feel good about this. I knew you would after a few weeks."

"What about you? Any prospects?"

"No, no." I glanced across the room, but didn't see him.

"Really? All this talk about marriage and you've barely dated anyone since I've known you."

"Sure I have. Just haven't lasted very long."

"You are too picky."

"I'm really not. It won't take much to sweep me off of my feet, but you've seen these last few guys. We had Mr. Baseball who probably looked into my eyes and saw baseballs in my pupils. Mr. Empty Pockets who would waste money on anything and everything, yet constantly talk about how he wanted to be rich. Mr. Suave who spent more time on his hair than I do. It's not like I've had the best options."

We laughed. I shrugged and looked around again.

Kate tapped the table and raised her eyebrows. "You seem anxious tonight. What's going on? You've seemed a little out there since your accident. Are you okay?"

I nodded.

"You ready to head out now?"

He must've left. "Yeah, I'm ready."

"Let me go to the bathroom real quick and we'll leave."

She hurried off while I picked up her receipt and turned it over. *My name is Ella. Call me sometime? 610-555-2949.* Immature is the best word to describe how I felt in that moment, but I didn't want to miss my chance. Something about him. I can't describe it. Something about the way he looked at me . . . I just knew.

# Ch. 8 | Matthew

Well, Gavin convinced me to let Lydia go if I genuinely wanted something different and new. I have to admit, I didn't like it. I know it sounds horrible, but I wanted to try something new while Lydia waited for me. I knew if I let her go that she'd end up with someone else quicker than I would. Her beauty, sense of humor, and intelligence would snatch any guy in a heartbeat.

She hated when I told her she could have any man in the world.

"I only want you," she'd say, wanting me to affirm the love she needed from me.

"I know." I'd stare into her eyes and wonder why I couldn't give my life to her and ask her to be my wife. She literally had everything I could ask for in a woman. Everything except *something*. Something I couldn't figure out for the life of me.

I do have issues. . . .

Enough of the issues. Gavin told me to stop hurting her, and I needed to let her go. I wrote her a letter. Explained my heart, why I needed to let her go, and that we could get together one last time and talk through it if she needed. It killed me to send that letter. I gave it to Gavin and, I hate to say, my eyes welled up when he walked out the door to the mailbox. I knew she wouldn't see me again. I knew the next time I'd see her she'd be wrapped around another guys arm.

Gavin said he'd help me find someone else and I needed to trust him. I hadn't the slightest idea what that meant, but I had nothing to lose. It didn't take long for him to reveal his plan.

He came in the apartment door smiling a little too much for my comfort.

"What are you up to?" I said, from my usual place on the couch.

"I've got your first prospect." He smiled again.

"My first prospect?"

"Friday, 8 o'clock. You are meeting her at Varalli's."

I stood up, probably looked like a deer on I-95.

"Don't look so shocked. You said you wanted to meet new people."

"No, no." I rubbed my head. "Not like this. Are you kidding me, Gavin? I'm not doing the blind date thing. I would rather see a woman on a street corner opposite of me and fall in love as we cross the street. I'm not into the blind dates, you know this. Why would you do this?"

"Don't overact. It will be fun. It's kind of like a game."

"A game? You wanted me to end things with Lydia because you thought I was playing with her heart, and now you want me to play with other women by creating a game show out of my life? I don't—"

"Calm down. I'm not asking you to be in a game show. I've got a few friends of friends and I thought this might give you a chance to see if you can find someone 'better' than Lydia."

"It's not about finding someone better." I sat back down.

Gavin shook his head and sat on the other couch.

"It's not. Look, I know I seem crazy, immature, whatever you want to call it. I know you think I'm so lucky to have Lydia and I'm nuts for letting her walk out the door, but I'm not out to find something better or worse or the same. I'm just curious about something different. What else is out there? Is there a one? Is Lydia the one? Is someone else?"

"Well, what if Lydia is the one and you let her go and don't find someone else?"

"I don't know." I pictured Lydia's face just before she left. Why that woman still loved me I will never know. "All I know is that if it's Lydia, she will wait for me and I will fall in love with her again. It will be like the beginning all over. If it's not her, then someone else will come. I don't doubt it."

"I can understand that."

"Thank you."

He looked down. Bright eyes gone serious again.

"What are you thinking?" I said.

"I'm thinking you think too much, man. I'm trying to live my life and you're always making me think too much about it."

Gavin rose and walked to the window. We've been friends so long, but you'd never know it if you met only one of us at a time. Gavin is one of those guys. Could get any girl he wants really. An artsy painter. Long hair that somehow looks messy and clean all at the same time. Casual meets professional is how I'd best describe his style. Me on the other hand? Short blonde hair. Paint brush in my pocket. Bruised knees and holes in my pants. Black Converse shoes with worn laces that never stay tied. I'm normal. Nobody wants the normal guy.

"What are you thinking?" I said.

He kept his eyes on something outside the window. "Nothing."

"The infamous nothing."

HE JUST HAD TO SET ME UP ON A BLIND DATE AT A restaurant. I could dress up too much, or dress down too much, and I had no idea what this girl would dress like. Gavin wouldn't tell me a thing about her. Oh, except her name. Chelsea. Given the name I imagined her to have blonde hair, curly, and dressed in a sundress with those cork board heels, or whatever they are.

So, I dressed to match a sundress with a button down shirt and the only nice jeans I own.

Gavin left earlier so I didn't have to hear his jokes as I left, thankfully. It didn't take long for me to get to the restaurant. An hour early.

Don't ask.

I brought a book in my shoulder bag and sat in the waiting area. I tried to read, but blind dates made me so nervous. I don't like the expectations that come with it. What if we are not attracted to each other? What if I'm attracted to her, but she thinks I'm weird? What if she thinks I chew too loud? What if she orders really expensive food?

Like I said, I tried to read, but that didn't go so well. I did, however, manage to fill the next hour with enough thoughts to send most people to their grave a few years too soon.

Then, about a half-hour before eight I started pacing in the waiting area. Hands in pockets, hands out. Leaning against the wall, sitting on the bench. Looking out the door out of the corner of my eye, turning around so she would only see my back. Very insane, very insane. Trust me, I know.

I looked at my phone. Quarter 'till eight.

"I'm not late, am I?" A soft female voice said from behind me.

I turned. Maybe I turned too fast.

"Are you Matt? You look like Matt."

"I do?" I smiled. Something about her casual nature eased my relentless mind.

She laughed. "Should we go in?"

"Sure." I opened the door for her and smelled a subtle honeysuckle scent as her blonde hair brushed my right arm.

No sundress. No curls. Soft blonde hair pulled back into a loose tie. Jeans. Not too tight. Not too loose. Plain white t-shirt. No makeup, at least none I could see. And topped off with a pair of white flip-flops. Normal, but pretty.

I kind of liked that.

The hostess seated us. I can't remember what she looked like. I was too busy looking at Chelsea. She reminded me of Lydia, only more natural. Lydia liked girly stuff. Makeup, curling her hair. I can't tell you how many days I spent sitting there watching her get ready for two hours, just so we could go to McDonald's.

We sat down across from each other. She smiled at me like she knew me for years. I smiled back. A pianist played in the background. I tried not to hear him.

"I love the music here," she said. "Have you been here before?"

"I've played piano here more times than I can count, but oddly enough I've never eaten here."

"Oh really? You play piano? Anything else?"

"I can fiddle with other things, but the piano is where I speak the most."

She laughed. "Speak?"

"Yeah." I picked up the menu and skimmed the pages.

"What do you mean by speak? How do you speak with an inanimate object?"

I looked up, then back to menu. "Well, I guess I use the keys to say what I'm feeling. The music sort of becomes my voice."

"Sounds weird." She picked up a menu. "So what do you like to eat?"

I tried to ignore the "sounds weird" part and looked at the prices in the menu. "I like anything, I guess. Not really picky. What about you?"

"I am a vegan. I only eat plants and things like that. Do you know how bad it is to eat meat? Oh, it's just horrible." She put her menu down and leaned forward. "You're not going to order meat, are you?"

"Does seafood count?"

She nodded, almost disgusted at me for even saying it.

"I was just kidding." I rubbed my neck and wondered what on earth I got myself into.

She looked at the menu. "Things like that aren't funny."

"Did you want to go somewhere else?"

"There's nothing on this menu that appeals to healthy people." She leaned back in her chair. "I can't believe you joked about that on a first date. That's so disrespectful."

The waiter stopped at our table. I held back a laugh.

"Sorry I took so long. I'm James. Can I get you two something to drink?"

"I'll have four bottles of wine and a cup of ice please," I said. "The biggest cup you have."

Arms crossed, Chelsea looked at the waiter and smiled. "Do you have distilled water?"

"Um . . . I'm afraid not. Just iced tap water with lemon or lime."

"No, thank you. I'd rather not have anything to drink then."

James looked at me, back to her, then at the floor. "I'm sorry ma'am. Are you sure I can't get you something to drink?"

"No, thank you. I'm not thirsty."

He looked back to me. "And you want four bottles of wine and a large cup of ice, right sir?"

"That would be correct."

"Okay, I'll be right back with that and I'll take your order for food then."

Chelsea looked away, anywhere but toward me, arms still crossed as tight as a guitar string about to pop.

"I like to drink." Took all I had not to laugh.

She stood up, without a single word. Arms red. Smile gone. And she left.

James brought the wine to me, I poured a glass, listened to the music for about a half-hour, and took the other three bottles home for later.

# Ch. 9 | Ella

Sarah and I enjoyed our time at the beach, but she couldn't wait to get home when I told her Dee planned to set me up on a blind date the following weekend. Who knows where Dee found this guy, but she assumed I would like him, and smiled at me as soon as I walked into *Chances* after my mini-vacation.

"That look is not encouraging." I walked behind the counter and looked at the envelope in Dee's hand. "What's that?"

"Oh, some guy dropped off his friend's work. They're just samples. He wants to sell some on the walls."

"We have so many of those. I don't want to say no to another person."

"Eh, we'll see." She opened the seal on the envelope. "So, are you ready for your big date?"

"Oh, I'm thrilled. Couldn't be more thrilled if I tried."

"Thought so." She sifted through the images in her hand. "Not bad. You might like these."

I took them from her. "If this date doesn't work, that's it. No more."

She laughed. "We'll see about that."

I looked at the images in my hand. "Are these copies of hand paintings?"

"Yeah, he wants to sell the originals though."

Dee took care of a few customers while I looked through the images. Something interesting about them. Unique. Then I saw something familiar.

"What?" Dee put some ice in a blender and poured coffee on top.

"These shoes." I ran my fingers across the image. Simple painting. Just a man sitting in a chair. Only his torso and below visible. Casually, he sat on a stool with his laces untied. "I remember these shoes from the coffee shop that night."

"What night? What shoes?"

"These black Converse shoes. I'm pretty sure he was wearing these shoes the night I saw him."

"You mean *the night? The him?*"

I nodded, eyes hugging tight to the picture.

"So you're saying this painter guy knows the man of your dreams?"

I laughed. "It's a long shot. Converse shoes are popular nowadays. I just didn't remember that detail until now."

"You want me to ask him if he can bring the guy in the painting to the shop?"

I rolled my eyes. "Please. Are you serious?"

"Can't hurt."

"No, don't bother with it. I doubt it's the same person. Just interesting, that's all. Who wears the same shoes for ten years? That's pretty unusual."

"Yeah." She whipped up another drink as she spoke. "You're probably right, but hey, if I see him again I'm definitely going to ask."

"You're too much." I topped off the drink with a generous helping of whipped cream.

"So, do you like the images?"

"Eh, they are nice. I'll keep them in the pile. Maybe when we need new ones I will give him a call. Right now we're pretty good. Too many starving artists in the world . . . I can't help them all unfortunately."

"Well, if it changes your mind at all, him and the friend who dropped them off were quite the lookers. And"—she held up her left hand—"no rings."

Waving her off, I headed to the back to do some paperwork.

SARAH KNOCKED ON THE BATHROOM DOOR. "WHAT ARE YOU getting ready for?"

"Nothing." I wrapped another lock of hair around the curling iron.

"You don't take that long most days. Got a big date?"

"Don't worry about it."

"Open up the door, eh?"

I unlocked the door and she came in.

"Wow, even breaking out the dusty curling iron." She leaned against the wall and watched me loosen a curl.

"Just a blind date. Dee set it up. I'm extremely nervous and extremely hesitant, but I'm doing it to prove to her that this is ridiculous."

"What if it ends up being someone just like the man you say all those years ago, but it's not him?"

"I don't even know what the guy from before is like . . . just what he looks like, or at least what he looked like then."

"Okay, so what if he looks like him, but isn't him? Will you give him a chance?"

I laughed. "It's not that complicated. I'm willing to meet other people, yeah. I'll give anyone a chance if it has promise, but it has to have promise."

She sat down on the floor by the bathtub, knees to her chest. "This guy I'm dating . . . ."

"Yeah?"

"He seems pretty serious."

I looked at her. She nodded. My gaze lingered on her left hand ring finger.

"No ring yet," she said. "But I think he may be looking now."

I raised my eyebrows. "That doesn't sound like excitement in your voice."

"I don't know." She stretched her legs out on the floor and pushed her cuticles back.

"What's going on?"

"This is so fast for me. I don't know if I can commit to someone yet."

"Sarah, we have to grow up one day. We're almost in our thirties. Pretty much all of our friends have nice husbands and little fenced in yards where their kids play. We're still single ladies living in the city."

"Believe me, I'm not complaining. You've just got me thinking about the Mr. Right stuff all the time. I really don't know. I didn't tell you much about him yet. There are some things that make me question what I'm getting myself into."

I finished putting on a light lip gloss and looked at her. "Do you love him, Sarah?"

"It's too soon to know the answer to that."

I smiled. "It's never too soon. Love grows, but it has to start somewhere."

She took a deep breath and exhaled. "Then maybe I don't."

"Is there something specific that's holding you back?"

"Yeah. I'm not sure I want to tell anyone though. It doesn't really paint him in the best light and I don't want to paint him blue if I do marry him. It could just be my own issues making him blue, when really he's green."

"Green, blue, red, purple. What are you talking about? Since when do you keep things from me?"

"This is different. It isn't my problem. I don't want you to see him in a negative light."

"What is it? Porn?"

She laughed. "Not sure about that one, but that's interesting. Why'd you bring that up of all things?"

"I don't know. That would be a red flag for me and pretty much every guy in the universe looks at it."

"Really? I never knew you didn't like porn."

"And you do?"

"Well, it doesn't do anything for me, but I wouldn't mind if my husband watched. As long as he comes home to me."

"That is the most unromantic thing I've ever heard of. What's with women always giving in to these horrible things men do? You are getting married to a person and I know I'm not perfect, but if I wanted other women in my marriage I wouldn't get married."

"That's one way to look at it, but another way to look at it is that it's just images, movies. They can't be attained. It's just fantasy land."

I finished my hair, sprayed it with some gunk, and looked at her. "Fantasy land easily turns into 900 numbers, and 900 numbers easily turn into strip joints, and strip joints easily turn into a quick fling with a prostitute. Next thing you know he'll be asking you to invite other women into your bedroom while the kids are sleeping in the next room."

"Highly doubt that. Most men are too wimpy to go that far."

"I don't know, Sarah. I wouldn't mess with a guy if he's openly into porn. That's asking for a tough time as a wife and mother."

"Well, you find me a guy who is 100% free of porn and I will marry him. How does that sound?"

"Deal."

IF I COULD THINK OF ONE WORD TO DESCRIBE HOW I FELT as I drove to meet my blind-date it would be . . . well, to be honest I have no idea. Nervous, excited, trying not to be excited, sad, happy. Did I say nervous? Pretty much a montage of emotions whirled into one haphazard state of being.

I stopped at a red light and wiped my hands on my skirt. By the time I reached for the steering wheel my hands were damp again.

Fifteen minutes too early, I pulled into the parking lot for the restaurant. Couldn't see anyone in the waiting area, so I drove to the back of the parking lot and waited. I felt more comfortable walking up to him than waiting for him to walk up to me. At least this way I could leave if I wanted.

Not that I'd really do that.

I think.

Two eternal minutes passed and I saw a black Passat park toward the front. A few seconds later a dark-haired nicely built man stepped out and I knew it had to be him. He fixed his simple button down shirt in the reflection of his car, then walked toward the restaurant. I watched for a few seconds to see if he would wait or go in. With a smile, he held the door for an older couple then walked inside the glass doors. I thought he walked in to be seated, but then he reappeared by the doors and looked at his watch.

He's going to think I'm so weird for parking this far back. I guess I deserve that.

"Well, here goes," I said to the steering wheel, and left my car for the first blind-date in my entire life.

Feeling about as silly as possible, I walked toward him. He came out of the doors and squinted in my direction with his hand above his eyes.

I walked toward him and he said, "Ella?"

"Yes. I'm sorry, but Dee never told me your name."

"Patrick." He reached out his hand and shook mine. "It's nice to meet you."

"You too."

He opened the door for me and followed behind. The hostess sat us immediately. We looked at each other across the table and didn't say much.

"You'll have to forgive me." He cleared the silence with his soft voice. "I'm not good with this type of thing."

"Don't worry. Neither am I."

An extremely beautiful waitress stopped by our table with her breasts practically touching my eye balls. Awkward to say the least.

"Hi. My name is Danielle. I will be taking care of you today. Our soups are special today." She caught her breath. "I mean, our soup specials today are broccoli and cheese, chicken enchilada, and dutch-style chicken pot pie. Can I get you guys something to use?"

I looked at Patrick. His eyes were practically glued to me.

"Did you want something?" I said to him.

"Oh, sorry." He looked at the girl, not her chest. Yes, I did notice.

"A drink, sir?"

"Water with lemon will be great, thank you."

She looked at me. "And you?"

"Same, please. Thank you."

"So," he said. "Dee didn't tell me much about you. To be honest, I thought she would set me up with someone a little on the punk rocker side."

I laughed. "Yeah. That's not quite me."

"No, not at all." He cleared his throat. "Not that there is anything wrong with that. I just think it would be too exciting of a lifestyle for me. That kind of music makes me want to crawl into a hole and go deaf."

"I know what you mean. It doesn't seem like music. More like unorganized noise."

"Exactly." He sipped his water.

I didn't even realize the waitress dropped our water off. I took a sip too.

He watched me. I watched him through the glass.

Smiling, he said, "What kind of music do you like?"

Flashbacks sliced through the present. "All sorts of things. I used to play violin, so I love pretty much anything with a violin in it. I like soundtracks, classical moody type of music. I like stuff like Ben Folds Five, Matchbox 20, then some older stuff like David Bowie, Queen. It's so hard for me to answer this question. I tend toward music that has an obvious melody. My best friend says I listen to depressing music, but I don't think so. Bohemian Rhapsody has emotion, but it's not depressing to me."

"I'm right there with you. I actually—"

"Are you two ready to order?" Our waitress popped back into the picture.

"Oh, forgive us," he said. "We haven't opened the menus yet."

"No problem." She snapped her pen. "I'll come back in a few minutes."

That's a good sign. Menus still closed on the table while our hearts were opening up to each other instead. What am I doing? I thought. I scooted back in my chair and looked down.

"You okay?" Patrick smiled. Something so sweet and innocent about his face. From a distance he looked so mature and manly, strong and defined. Up close he still looked his age, early-thirties probably, but the way the lines under his eyes pulled up his smile made me feel like a kid again.

"I'm okay." I tried to sit still. "Something about this just seems so weird to me. I always wanted to fall in love in an unexpected way. To meet someone across the coffee shop and end up talking until the sun wakes us out of our stupor. This is so unnatural to me."

"Maybe that makes it unexpected."

"That it's unnatural?" I smiled. "That's a good point."

"I never thought I'd be here either. This is honestly the hardest thing I've ever done in my life."

"Really?"

He looked away, across the restaurant, dazed. "Yeah. I just don't feel ready. And I like you. And that makes me even more nervous."

"Well, if it makes you feel any better . . . I feel the exact same way."

The lines around his eyes creased again, lifting his lips into that child-like smile. *Did I just tell him I liked him? I didn't mean to say that. I can't believe I just said that.*

"We better look at the menu," he said, opening to glossy images of artistically arranged steak and chicken.

I opened mine and, well, nothing appealed to my stomach except a reprieve from the butterflies flapping around inside of me.

"You know," he said. "Nothing is really standing out to me. How about we go get ice cream instead?"

My heart smiled along with my face. I couldn't believe the way I felt. Excited. Nervous. The way it felt to look into a man's eyes and actually feel that promise . . . could this really be happening to me without the coffee shop mystery man? Could someone else be my one? Or could there really be many choices in a sea of fish, and I just had to pick one for me?

He led me outside and we decided to take his car.

"Excuse the mess." He opened the passenger door and shoved a few papers into the backseat. "I always have papers in my car. I'm not the most organized."

"What do you do for a living?"

He held up his hand, motioning for me to wait. Then he walked around the car, got in beside me, and put the keys in the ignition. "I don't like answering this question."

"That bad, huh?"

He laughed as he backed up, his hand about two inches from my shoulder. "I'm a chiropractor."

"What's wrong with that?"

"Well, when I tell most people I'm a chiropractor they think I am rich. Fact is, I own my own place, just started it, and even when I worked for someone else I made less than thirty-thousand a year."

"Money isn't important." I looked out the window. "Neither is loving what you do. Honestly, jobs are jobs. Even the things we love the most become just that . . . a job. There's always a negative or a stress when you have to do something to make money, instead of pure enjoyment."

"That's true." He stopped at a red light and looked at me.

I looked away, unable to handle his penetrating eyes. My emotions were leading my mind. Not used to it. I didn't like it. Part of me wanted to get out of the car immediately, but I must have enjoyed some part of it. It felt like falling in love, something I waited so long to experience. How could I know he is the one? How could I know whether to let myself fall in love with him?

He accelerated the car and I looked at him. Handsome, to say the least.

He looked at me. I looked away.

"You wanna go to *More than Just Ice Cream* on Locust Street?" he said.

"That sounds nice." I smiled. "I love their—"

"I love their Candy Land flavor."

"Wow. That's exactly what I was going to say."

Within a few minutes we were standing in line for ice cream. He stood so close to me I could smell his cologne. Light and clean with a hint of citrus. Made me want to lean in closer.

He ordered two exact ice cream dishes. We moved over to the register and I pulled out my wallet. Gently, he held my hand and put it back into my purse.

"Ladies never pay," he said.

Butterflies. The warmth of his touch lingered on my skin.

AFTER ICE CREAM WE WENT TO A LOCAL PARK AND SAT UNDER the long arms of an oak tree. I took off my shoes, he took off his flip-flops, and we leaned back on the tree trunk together. Everything with him happened so naturally. I couldn't wait to tell Sarah. She would never believe I let go of my analytical brain for a few hours and actually enjoyed myself. I couldn't believe it either.

Hours passed. Literally like minutes. We talked about everything from music to what kind of houses we like. The time went too fast, spinning us right into the next morning.

Patrick looked at his cell phone. "You won't believe this."

"What?" I smiled. "Is it almost sunrise?"

"Not quite, but close. It's four in the morning. I haven't done this in years."

"I don't know if I've ever stayed up this late." I rubbed my eyes. "And I have to work tomorrow."

"You mean today."

"Yes, thanks for the reminder."

He looked at me. Silly grin turned serious. We sat close all night, often touching arms or legs, but he never tried to kiss me. The thought made me nervous. I promised myself my lips would never touch another man's lips until I knew it was the one I'd marry.

I looked away. His fingers brushed my hand, finally resting on top of my fingers. I looked back to his dark eyes.

"I'm sorry." He squeezed my hand. "I really want to kiss you."

I nodded and smiled. He touched my chin and made me look at him again.

"This is so hard for me," he said. "It's been a while since she died, but I never thought I'd fall in love again, much less desire it as much as I do now."

I looked down at our locked fingers. She? He brought up a she in the middle of a perfect first kiss moment? Dee never mentioned a she.

"I'm sorry." He squeezed my hand again. "Did I say too much? Are you not interested at all?"

I tried to smile. "You didn't say too much."

"Dee told you about my wife, didn't she?"

I raised my eyebrows. The she is a wife. Speechless, I stared at him, but he said nothing. I put on my shoes. Patrick did as well. The previously married man that I almost let myself kiss. I stood and he reached for my hand. I moved over.

"Patrick," I said. "I have to be honest with you. I saw a guy in a coffee shop when I was younger. It's been years since then, but I think about him every day. Dee set me up on this date because, well, I guess because she knew you and I would like each other."

He nodded. "I haven't felt like this in a long time."

"You are a great guy. Attractive, sweet, funny, smart, and creative. You are everything I'd ever ask for in a husband. Of course we don't know each other well, but I could have easily given my heart to you after this first night."

He nodded, a mixture of sadness and excitement painted in his brown eyes. "I think that's a description of a nice man, but not this one."

"And add humble on top of that. Listen"—I took a breath—"I have loved this guy I've never met for the last few years. I've promised myself I would wait for him and never give my heart to another person. I know I'm probably crazy and maybe I'll never meet him. Maybe there isn't one person. Maybe soul-mates don't exist. I don't know, Patrick. I honestly don't know. What I do know is that my heart belongs to that man across the coffee shop, and yours belongs to your wife."

"Everyone tells me I need to move on. I understand your point and your desire to wait for this other man, but what if you never meet him? I know I will never bring my wife back to life. She's lying in the ground right outside of Philly."

My eyes watered. "You are lonely. I am, too. But that doesn't change the fact that you have a wife and I have a husband. Just because we can't kiss them doesn't mean they don't exist."

"You don't think I should move on?"

The ivory moonlight emphasized the tears in both of our eyes. "I don't think you should. You just referred to her as your wife. You didn't say ex-wife. Go put your ring back on. Stay faithful to her even now. There is only one and you found her. Just because life took her too soon doesn't mean you have to take her out of your own life."

"That seems impossible."

"It does. And I won't blame you if you get married again. I know I'm idealistic. I know I'll probably spend the rest of my life single, but I'd rather be single forever than married to someone else. Maybe this was meant to happen so that I could see that. Maybe it was meant to happen so that you could see it, or just to know that you can fall in love again if you want to."

"This has been the most interesting night of my life, hands down."

I laughed. "I agree."

We walked back to his car and drove back to the restaurant in silence. We exchanged phone numbers at the end, gave each other a warm hug, and I even gave him a kiss on the cheek.

"Keep in touch," he said. "I want to know if you ever find this man. He is one extremely lucky guy. Your story should be in the news. I've never heard anything like it."

"Thanks." I laughed. "Well, it won't be worth the news if I end up single until I'm ninety."

"Yes it will." He smiled. "Trust me, it will."

# Ch. 10 | Matthew

"What were you thinking?" I said to Gavin as we walked down the busy city street toward coffee and deliciousness.

He laughed. "She seemed nice. I had no idea it would be that bad."

"Bad doesn't do it justice, Gavin."

He laughed again.

"I'm serious, and you expect me to go out this weekend with another one?" I shook my head and squeezed his shoulder. "Don't think so, man. You couldn't pay me."

"You'll go. I promise this one will be better."

"I'm not doing it. No more blind-dates. Just let it go and if I'm meant to find someone, that's great. If not, that's wonderful. Blind-dates don't work."

"What if I allow you to set me up on a blind-date too?"

"Yeah. I can count the amount of girls I know on one hand, and they're married. Being with someone for the last few years didn't give me much time to meet single women."

"Which is good." He opened the door to *Chances*. "How about this . . . I will try a dating site and you will go on another blind-date."

I followed him into the cafe. The sweet aroma of chocolate cake and coffee found its way to my wallet. We only intended to come in and check on his paintings, but by the time I got to the counter I already mentally ate an entire slice of triple chocolate cake.

"You getting something?" Gavin said.

"Yeah. And about the blind-date thing . . . no, thanks."

A young man, probably just out of high school, stood at the register.

"Can I get you guys something?"

"I'll get a piece of that cake, and also an iced caramel latte." I handed him a twenty.

Gavin looked around. "Is the owner here?"

"No," the guy said. "She was supposed to be here this morning, but she called and said she'll be in later this afternoon."

"Okay, thank you." Gavin glanced at the walls. "I gave her some of my art to look at and wanted to check and see what she thought about it."

"Can you come back this afternoon? She will be here then. I'm new here and don't know much about the art."

"I can try." Gavin said, then turned to me. "You going to be around tonight? Maybe we can come back for the live music and have a talk about your future dates."

The cashier guy gave me a brown paper bag and my coffee. We nodded, thanked him, and walked outside and toward our apartment.

"I have a job later, but you should definitely come. This would be a great opportunity for you." I sipped the refreshing latte and scarfed down the cake in two bites.

"Whoa." Gavin smiled. "Would you like me to go buy you another piece?"

I grinned a chocolatey grin. "I'm good, but you should get one for yourself tonight. I can't even describe how good that was."

"Weird that we used to work there. It looks like a completely different place."

"Tastes like a completely different place, too."

GAVIN AND I PASSED TIME PLAYING MUSIC TOGETHER UNTIL he left to meet the *Chances* owner and I went to check out a new job site. Normally I did consultations during the day, but this woman worked at home during the day and preferred me to come later. Evening it is, I said to myself as I drove out of the city and into Collingswood, a nice little suburban area in Philly.

I pulled into her driveway and gathered my papers and paint sample books, then walked up to her door and knocked.

No answer. .

I ruffled my papers a little, looked at my watch, and knocked again.

A few seconds passed and the door opened.

"Oh, hey," she said, her bright eyes catching the sun. "You must be Matt. Sorry, I had music on as I was cleaning and didn't realize you were knocking. You weren't standing here too long, were you?"

I smiled. "No. Just a few seconds. It's no problem at all."

She pulled the headphones out of her ears. I heard Ben Folds Five before she turned her iPod off. "You can come in and have a seat."

I followed her to the living room. "It's not every day I hear of someone listening to Ben Folds as their cleaning."

She motioned for me to sit on the couch across from the chair she sat down in. "I know, I know. Not the most pick-me-up song in the world, but I love singing with him. It actually does motivate me in a weird way."

I looked behind her at the bare walls and into the empty dining room. "So, did you just move in?"

"Actually," she said, looking around her, "I've been here for a year now. Hard to believe, I know."

"You are looking to paint every room in the house?" I really didn't think she could afford it. She barely had any furniture except the couch and chair we were sitting on.

I tried not to notice her beauty as she pulled her hair into one of those messy hair things women do. She looked around again, silent. I watched her. Looked as though she were calculating things in her mind.

A slight smile hid behind her teeth. "My husband and I moved here one year ago. Our first home together." She put her hand on her stomach and took a deep breath. "He always wanted to paint the house, but I kept saying we couldn't afford it. So now I want to surprise him and have the entire house painted."

"And he doesn't know?"

"Well, he died a month ago." She held her stomach again. "I'm seventeen weeks pregnant with our first baby."

I nodded, unsure of what to say. I mean, what do you say to a beautiful woman who is seventeen weeks pregnant with her dead husband's child?

"It's okay," she said. "I know it's hard to find words. It doesn't make sense to me either. Andy always wanted to fix up the house. He worked so hard to buy this house and when we finally moved in we could barely afford food, much less furniture and paint and new floors."

"Yeah, well if it makes you feel any better I'm older than you and I live in an apartment with my best friend from high school."

She laughed, her gorgeous smile accentuating her lips. Definitely could be a model. Definitely.

"At least I'm assuming I'm older than you," I said. "Probably the safest assumption I could make, huh?"

"I'm twenty-four," she said. "We were married when I was twenty-one. Took us three years to get this place and then we got pregnant. I never expected to be alone right now."

"What happened to Andy?"

She looked down.

"I'm sorry. I said too much." I pulled out the paint samples. "Do you want to go over some color samples?"

"No, you didn't ask too much. It's just hard for me to remember that this is not a dream. My husband really died."

"I'm really sorry, Heidi. I don't know what to say."

"It's okay." She sniffed a little. "He was killed by a drunk driver on his way home from work. At three in the afternoon. Can you believe someone was already drunk at that point? I've sent him letters."

Silence.

"I figured only someone with their own problems could be drunk at three in the afternoon. And after killing someone? I hope he doesn't lose his mind and kill himself too."

We both looked at each other. I couldn't believe it. This beautiful, young wife already a widow and soon-to-be single mother, genuinely concerned about the drunk guy that crashed into the man she married. It's not every day you meet someone like her.

"I was on the phone with him when it happened," she said, eyes blurry.

I nodded, realizing my own mortality.

"The last sound I remember is that deathly car crash sound. You know, screeching tires against asphalt, the bang of a collision, and glass shattering everywhere. Then the phone died. I immediately left the house, running barefoot. We only had one car at the time and I work from home." She shook her head. "I ran and ran until I finally found him, only a mile from the house. When I finally reached the car the sirens were getting closer. I didn't see him anywhere. Nowhere in the car or anywhere around it. We had an old car. The driver's side seatbelt stopped worked shortly before our emissions test. It was one of those shoulder belts that slides along the car door with a separate lap belt. I begged him to get it fixed.

"Anyway, I screamed at the top of my lungs. I just screamed his name over and over and over again. Then I ran to the other car. No one there either. That's when I saw him. My heart literally felt numb. Across the street I could see his arms twisted behind his head. His femur sticking out of his thigh. Clothes stained red. With more red pouring out and making a puddle around him. I ran to him. Knelt beside him and forced his eyes open. I've seen a lot of expressions on his face, but there's nothing like seeing someone lifeless. His eyes looked straight ahead. Face relaxed. Jaw dropped and drool mixed with blood pouring onto his collar."

I took a deep breath.

"Anyway." She wiped her eyes. "I said too much. I didn't mean to overwhelm you with my tragic story. You've only been here five minutes. I'm so sorry."

"No, no." I shook my head. "I understand. I'm glad you could get some of that out again. I can't imagine what you must be going through."

"It's hard," she said. "My family lives in Virginia and I have no friends here. I moved here for him. His parents don't like me, never have. They even blame me for his death and refuse to talk to me, save the occasional email to ask how the prenatal appointments are going. They want me to name the child Andrea or Andrew after him. They told me I'd be a horrible mother not to, but Andy hated that. He never wanted a child named after him. He wanted them to have their own unique name. But I know there is good in this. There's always good in every circumstance. Just depends on how we look at things."

"I guess that's true."

"And no, I didn't mention all of this to get free paint."

We both hid our pain and confusion with a laugh. I couldn't help but cringe when I imagined this young, pregnant newlywed holding her mangled husband's body in a ditch. The pain she must have been enduring seemed unbearable to me. And I thought I had problems.

I spent the next three hours at her house. Neither of us could believe it. We walked through each room and as we talked about colors she told me more of her story. She had a personal reason for every color she chose. I didn't mind hearing her talk. Something about her I enjoyed. She brought me peace. And it wasn't that she was so beautiful I had to consciously tell myself not to be attracted to her. It wasn't that at all. It was the beauty inside of her that affected me so much. How many women lose their husband, paint an entire house all sorts of meaningful colors from their relationship, and talk to the paint guy without a single hint of flirtation?

I liked her, in a completely non-romantic way. Part of me couldn't wait to come back and paint the house. It wasn't a small house. Not big either, but enough rooms to keep me busy for a few weeks. Most of my clients aren't home when I paint, but she worked from home. I couldn't wait to get to know her better.

I know it's hard to believe, but I really didn't think of her as a potential date. In fact, she wouldn't allow it. She twirled her rings and talked about Andy as though he were still alive. I know why, too. It became so clear by the time I left our consultation.

He never died to her.

# Ch. 11 | Ella

Another day in the coffee shop, another strange day in the life of Ella Rhodes. Dee sat in my office, across from me, staring at me like I had lost my mind.

"I know it's unrealistic of me," I said as she leaned back in the chair across from me. "But I know what I said to Patrick was right. I could never forgive myself for marrying someone who fell in love and watched his bride walk down the aisle just a few years earlier. One bride is enough for every man. If one bride isn't enough, then why bother with faithfulness anyway?"

"Ella, Ella, Ella." She stood and sighed. "You live in a dream world."

"What's so dreamy about that?"

She walked to the door. "Who has the desire, much less the strength, to marry only one person in their lifetime? What about people who are abused? Or Patrick? There is a such thing called *until death parts us.* You really expect him to stay faithful to his dead wife even if he lives until he is a hundred years old?"

I nodded.

"No one lives like that. It's unheard of. You're missing a perfectly good man because you think he should only have one wife in his lifetime. How do you know if she was the infamous one? What if she had to die so he could meet someone else?"

"I don't know, Dee. You're getting too deep for me. I don't sit around and think through logistics. I know what I feel doesn't make sense. I know my life doesn't make sense. But maybe that's exactly what I want. Maybe I don't want to live by sense. Maybe I want to live by love . . . love that is unheard of. Love that stays faithful, even if death parts us."

Dee rolled her eyes with a smile. "You are a fascinating person. I've met my fair share of fascinating people, but you are definitely unique in your own way. I think you live in a world no one else has ever found, and probably never will. You're going to be lonely forever if you don't get your head out of the clouds."

"The man I marry will live in this crazy world of mine with me."

Summer walked into my office and smiled. "Sorry, I don't mean to interrupt, but there is a man here to see you about paintings or something."

"Thanks, Summer. Do you know what his name is?"

"No, but he said he talked to Dee and dropped his stuff off for you to review. He's been here several times trying to talk with you."

Dee laughed. She knew I didn't like dealing with the starving artists. I felt so bad telling them I didn't have room for their work. Truth is I had stacks and stacks of people who wanted their work in here. I couldn't give everyone a chance and I am not a fan of crushing dreams. I had enough crushed dreams of my own.

"I'll tell you what," I said to Summer. "Tell him to bring in three of his favorite paintings. I will put them up and we'll see how it goes."

She smiled and left the office.

Dee looked at me. "I'm shocked."

"I know. Honestly, I just didn't want to get up. I have too much work to do and the last thing I want to do is tell someone else I can't help them sell their art right now."

"That guy's determination paid off. Is he the one with the Converse shoes friend?"

I laughed. "I believe so."

"Things could get interesting around here in the Ella Rhodes story."

"The Ella Rhodes story is right. Not sure about interesting. Maybe in a strange way."

She laughed and walked out of my office. Time to catch up on the one thousand phone calls and papers I needed to sort through. What I would give to leave all of this to be a wife and stay-at-home mother. Now, that's dreaming.

"COME ON," DEE SAID AS SARAH WAITED FOR ME AT THE FRONT door of the shop. "Just one more date. I promise he is really nice and he has no ex-wives."

Sarah smiled.

I shrugged my shoulders. "What am I going to do with you people?"

"Please," Dee said.

Sarah leaned against the door. "What could it hurt?"

"It could hurt some guy who wants a date and I don't. I really am content being single. I've gotten used to it."

Dee turned off the lights and we met Sarah at the front door. Carried by silence, we walked outside and inhaled the stuffy city air.

"I miss the beach," I said. "This air is suffocating."

"I agree." Sarah walked toward the corner.

Dee and I followed.

"I have to go this way." Dee tapped my shoulder. "We'll talk later."

"Yeah, we'll see about that. Have a good night, Dee. See you in the morning."

Sarah and I walked to our apartment. She never said a word. I didn't notice until we went inside and she plopped on the couch, staring off into space.

"Everything okay?" I inched toward her.

"Yeah, why?"

"You are quieter than usual. Not your typical joyful self."

She shrugged. "I don't know how much I want to say yet. It could be nothing."

"What? Did something happen with your mystery man?" I leaned back and cushioned my head with a pillow. "When am I going to meet him?"

"Oh. He's the least of my concerns right now."

"Sounds romantic. So, what's going on then?"

"With him? Nothing. Just taking it day-by-day. He is a little too intense for me though."

"Too intense? For you?"

"He is just very clingy. I don't know. It's weird when someone wants to marry you two days into meeting you. It takes me a little longer to know."

"Well, when it's the right one I believe you know in an instant. You could know that person for years, be their best friend in preschool through college, but suddenly one day you look at him and you think to yourself, 'He is my person,' and you know in that instant you are going to marry him. For some people it can happen the second they meet, for others years after loathing each other, but either way I think it's this magical moment that happens to us and we just know."

"Yes. The whimsical dream land of Ella." She smiled. "That would be nice, but really, what are the chances?"

"I named my cafe *Chances* for a reason."

"Yes. Yes, you certainly did."

"You never told me what's bothering you if it isn't mystery man."

"We'll talk about it later. It's too much for me to think about it."

LATER THAT NIGHT I GOT COMFORTABLE IN BED AND PICKED up *Sense and Sensibility*. One paragraph into the second chapter and I heard a whimper. Quiet, I listened a few minutes as the gentle humming of the central air conditioner filled the air, but no whimper. A few sentences later, I heard it again. Sounded like someone outside of my window.

I walked to the window, opened it, and looked around. Nothing. No sad people. Only the rushing cars and sounds of a busy city that never sleeps.

I went back to my bed, got comfortable, and continued reading.

*A continuance in a place where everything reminded her of former delight was exactly what suited her mind. In seasons of cheerfulness, no temper could be more cheerful than hers, or possess, in a greater degree, that sanguine expectation of happiness which is happiness itself. But in sorrow she must be equally carried away by her fancy, and as far beyond consolation as in pleasure she was beyond alloy.*

A soft cry interrupted Jane Austen.

Again, I rose from bed and walked into the hallway.

Sarah.

I inched toward her door and tapped. "You okay, Sarah?"

She sniffed. The mattress creaked. "I'm okay. We'll talk later."

I knew better. If Sarah didn't want to talk about something she really didn't want to talk about something. If someone asked me I would respond the same way, except I'd really want them to pry it out of me. For some odd reason. "Leave me alone" in my world really means "beg me to tell you."

Not Sarah. I knew her long enough to know she would tell me when she's ready. Can't say I liked that about her. I have this need-to-know personality. If someone is hurting, especially someone close to me, I feel like I need to know the details and my brain will create five-thousand scenarios much worse than reality as I wait for them to tell me what's going on.

Mom always told me to be a writer. She said I had a writer's way of looking at life. I analyze people constantly. And everything in my mind is always a little better or worse than the way others see it. I also have a weird habit of imagining my funeral and picturing the most horrible things, like cutting an orange only to trip and send the knife through my chest.

Morbid. Mom always called me morbid. I have no idea why my brain conjured these images, but I could never be a writer. Music is my passion and I have absolutely no talent when it comes to writing. I feel like every talent is a gift. Sometimes the gift needs a lot of practice before we realize that it's a talent we possess, for others it comes naturally from birth, but either way it's a gift we're either born with or not. Music is that gift for me, not writing.

Although, I devour books like you wouldn't believe.

Cuddling under my covers, I opened *Sense and Sensibility* and tried to ignore the cries echoing from my best friend's room. All I could think is her new love interest abused her. She didn't act this way often, and it seemed to be triggered from his entrance into her life.

I tried to focus on the words in the book again, but I ended up with the pages sprawled on my stomach and my eyes on the speckles of moonlight dancing on the ceiling. Sarah, my sensible sister. And me, the sense-filled dreamer. I've read this book a thousand times over. I don't know why. The ending didn't appeal to me, I have to admit. Of course I cry every time Edward comes back for Elinor, but did Willoughby really have to choose himself over love? Did Marianne really have to marry Colonel Brandon?

Will that be the story of my life? Or will I find a Willoughby willing to sacrifice himself for true love? Willing to change and let go of his personal desires?

I skipped to the end of the book and read.

*Marianne Dashwood was born to an extraordinary fate. She was born to discover the falsehood of her own opinions, and to counteract, by her conduct, her most favourite maxims.*

Perhaps, I wondered, I needed to be the one to change.

# Ch. 12 | Matthew

I showed up at Heidi's house with three gallons of golden honey paint. She opened the door and smiled. Faded jeans, over-sized t-shirt hanging off her bare shoulder, and hair framing her face in messy waves.

She sighed and blew at her hair. "Sorry. I seem to take forever when you knock on the door."

"Everything okay?"

She motioned for me to walk in, then closed the door as I stepped beside her. "I'm okay. Just a little bit of a procrastinator. Wanted to get the room ready for you like you asked."

"No problem. You've got a lot on your plate." I set the paint down in her living room. "Hey, I gotta run out and get my ladder and some other things."

"Need some help?"

I looked at her stomach. "Can you carry things with a baby?"

She laughed. "I'll be okay. I can help carry something light."

We walked out together with only the sound of crickets around us. I handed her some plastic sheets, paint trays, and rollers. Paint brushes already in my pockets, I picked up the ladder and we made our way back to the house.

"Do you mind if I paint, too?" she said.

"Well, I would normally never let a client do that for many reasons, especially a pregnant one, but since you chose VOC-free paint and you have special circumstances . . . yes, I'd be glad to have your help."

Took me twenty minutes to prepare the room when Heidi came in with her iPod hooked up to a small stereo.

"What kind of music do you like?" She pressed a few buttons.

"All kinds." I poured some paint into a tray. "Surprise me."

"How about I surprise myself too and do an iPod shuffle with all the songs?"

"Sounds good to me. You can pick up that roller there and we'll get this wall painted, just don't expect it to be perfect since you're helping."

She raised her eyebrows, trying to hold back a smile, but failing. Matchbox 20 *I'll Believe You When* drummed its way into our conversation.

"Love this song." I soaked my roller with paint and brushed it along the wall in front of me.

"Really? A lot of guys I know don't admit they like Matchbox 20."

"What's wrong with 'em? I mean, some of their stuff is a little on the fluffy side, but they've got some great songs. Especially the *Exile on Mainstream* album."

"I love that you call them albums still."

Her hair fell into her face as she dipped a roller into the paint. I tried not to notice, telling myself I couldn't like this woman, this pregnant widowed woman.

She looked up, eyes peeking through strands of hair. "What do I do?"

If the situation were different I might've been tempted to take her hand and show her. Who am I kidding? I was tempted and it really bothered me.

In her mind, I reminded myself, she's taken. Last thing I wanted to do is take her from him. I always told myself I'd never be that guy, whether the other guy is alive or not.

"You okay?" she said, arm still holding the doused roller.

"It's pretty easy. I know you aren't expecting perfection here, so just put it on there and start rolling. You'll find a natural rhythm. Here"—I added another layer of honey over the white wall—"watch what I do and follow me."

She rolled along with me. Obviously she had never painted before in her life. Awkward strokes, stiff arm, beautiful face.

*Stop, Matt,* I told myself. Again. *She's taken. And vulnerable. And you're being ridiculous.*

"Who's being ridiculous?" She stopped painting.

"Oh, um, I was just saying . . . um, it might be ridiculous, but if you try to paint along to the music you'll kinda go with the flow. It'll feel more natural that way. I always paint to music, unless I'm in a weird mood."

"What constitutes a weird mood?"

"Oh, you know, depressed or overly analytical."

"You are so funny. I don't think I've met a guy like you before."

"Kind of like there's only one Jim Carey in the world and he doesn't go down in the books as most wanted for a nice romantic date, now does he?"

She laughed and found her rhythm to the next song. We painted and listened, enjoying the music as her living room walls turned from bright white hospital walls to honey-dipped ice cream cones.

"You know"—she saturated her roller again—"I chose this color for this room because it was the color of my bedroom when I first met Andy."

I looked at her as I moved on to the next wall.

"I lived with my parents until we got married. One night, I think it was after our third or fourth date, I asked him to come in for a second to listen to a tape I recorded. The song was written to my future husband. I wanted to play it for him, because even on our fourth date I knew I'd marry him."

"Wow." I tried not to notice her glassy eyes.

"So, when I started to play the tape he turned it off and said, 'I want to hear you play it, right now.' My stomach tied up in a zillion knots. I never played live for anyone. Only sang and strummed for a dinky recording thing plugged into my outdated stereo."

Smiling, I pictured the exact scene. I probably owned the same dinky recorder. "So, did you play for him?"

"Of course. How could I resist his charming smile?" She touched her lips. "He sat on the floor, crossed his legs. I got my guitar and sat on my bed so I wouldn't be directly across from him on the floor. I was so, so embarrassed. For the life of me, I couldn't play. He laughed and told me to turn around and face the opposite wall, so I did."

She paused, held back tears.

I stopped painting and waited for her to continue.

"Sorry, it's so hard to think of him knowing I'll never kiss him again."

I reached for her shoulder, then stopped. My empty hand dangled next to her empty hand.

"So, I played for him. I ended up so into it that my eyes were closed and when I opened them he was on his knees in front of me. We spent our first few dates mesmerized with each other in that giddy way, but this time he looked at me with such seriousness on his face. I'm sure I blushed. All I know is I felt more comfortable than ever before, but couldn't put words to it until he said, 'Heidi, my love, I'm finally home.' We kissed, soft and sweet, but more romantic than our first kiss. When we stopped kissing he looked at the wall to the left of us and said, 'I want to paint our living room this color so we always remember what it felt like when we found our true home.'"

A tear tripped off her nose and fell to her top lip. She licked it off and wiped her cheeks with her forearm, then looked up at me. "I feel so crazy talking to you like this. My painter. I hope I don't scare you off. It means a lot to me that you're willing to help me do this. It means more than you'll ever know."

"Sounds like he was a pretty amazing man."

"He was the most amazing." She held up her left hand. "This ring will never leave my finger. I'll never find someone who is worth taking this ring off."

My mind darted words around like arrows missing their marks.

"On that note," she said, "let's get painting."

"Do you mind if I ask you a question?"

"Sure. I'm not one to hide things, as you can tell."

"How do you find a love like that?" I looked away, focused on my paint roller again. "See, I have this problem with feeling like there is only one person for me in this world. Just one woman in a world of millions. The only problem is I don't know if I'll ever find her."

"I think you will."

"But how do you know when you have found the one?"

She paused *Tiny Dancer*. "Sorry, can't think when that song is on. Makes me want to sing every time."

I nodded.

"Well, I don't know how to answer that. Maybe it's different for everyone. For us, we just knew immediately. I don't think that's the case for everyone. My brother fell in love with a girl he went to high school with. They sat next to each other during their entire senior year and barely talked, unless it had to do with school work. Neither of them were attracted to each other at first. Just two completely different people. He was a jock, she was nowhere near a cheerleader. Five years later they accidentally ran into each other, literally, at the grocery store and they've been together since."

"Can I ask you another question?"

"Of course."

"All of this sounds romantic, but where's the reality?"

"You mean the fights and disagreements?"

"Yeah. Tell me that exists, because I can't imagine ever having one of these fairy tale romances."

She smiled. "It exists. Andy and I disagreed about what to spend our money on when we first moved here. We disagreed on baby names. Many things. But I guess when you love someone more than you love yourself you will sacrifice your desires for them. You end up wanting them to be happy even at the cost of your own desires. Actually, your happiness becomes making them happy."

"Interesting how you just made something painful sound so romantic."

"That's just it. With Andy and me . . . the pain was romantic because it was part of our story, part of us growing into one person. My books became ours, not mine. Was it easy? Not at all. Did we sometimes make each other cry? Of course. But in the end these rings stayed on our fingers and we made a pact to never fall asleep in separate rooms."

"Sounds simple enough."

"You'll find her, Matthew." She turned the music back on. "Now, let's get this first coat finished."

GAVIN RUBBED HIS EYES. "YOU MEAN TO TELL ME YOU ARE falling for a widow who wants nothing to do with falling in love with someone else?"

"There you go. You're reading into things again." I opened the refrigerator and grabbed a sprite. "I'm saying she is beautiful in this way I've never seen before. She is sticking by this guy no matter what. She knows she is beautiful and could get married again if she wanted to, even if she had ten kids, but she is not interested. I have to constantly remind myself to not be attracted to her because this love she lives is magnetic. It makes her more beautiful than she already is."

"Interesting situation you have found yourself in."

"It's definitely weird, man." I opened the sprite and took a sip. "Really weird."

"So, what are you going to do?"

"Nothing at all. She is cute and sweet, but never flirts with me at all. She never sends the message that she's interested. She only talks about him. Get this. She told me she will never take her wedding ring off because no man will ever be worth it."

"Wow."

"Exactly."

"Yeah . . . wow."

"She's young. She's only twenty-four or five, can't remember. An entire life ahead of her, a baby inside, and she's going to do all of this without a man because the only one worth marrying is still alive to her."

"Maybe that will fade with time and she'll reconsider."

"Oh, come on. Don't give up so easily."

He leaned against the side of the refrigerator and crossed his legs. "I'm just being honest. It could happen."

"I want to find a love like that. I want to find a woman who loves me like that, and a woman I love like that."

"Me too, Matt."

"So you do think it's possible?"

"Of course." He walked toward the living room. "Just hard to imagine sometimes."

I followed. "Do you think you will settle if you don't find that?"

"I don't know. This isn't the central part of my life. I'm going one day at a time here. Whatever happens, happens."

"I don't buy it."

"Buy what?"

"You haven't been the same since your last breakup. It still gets to you. I know you think about love more than you let on."

"We're men. Come on, now. Do we have to talk like we're women all the time?"

I laughed. "You're probably right."

"Anyway, I'd like to come and paint this house with you sometime. Maybe next Tuesday since I have nothing to do. I really want to hear this girl's story.'"

"I don't think she'll mind at all." I finished my soda and bent the cap off. Weird habit. "Oh, by the way, I know you think about this stuff as much as I do, you just don't want to talk about it because it upsets you."

He shook his head. "Go play the piano or something."

# Ch. 13 | Ella

Dee begged me to go on another blind date. Every time I saw her it's the first thing she said, the last thing she said when I left, and pretty much the only thing she said during our time together.

"Here." She came into my office and handed me a large rectangular box.

"What's this?"

"Converse shoes dropped them off this morning for his friend."

"You are too much."

"What?" She walked to the door. "He's cute."

"Let me guess." I opened the box and pulled out three framed paintings. "Is Converse shoes guy the one you asked to go on a blind date with me?"

She waved her finger in the air. "Now, there's an idea."

She left the office in a hurry. Must've been busy out there. Dee is nothing short of a sweet person. Real, compassionate, and not as intimidating as she comes across, but why did people in relationships always seem to think every single person around them should be in a relationship as well?

I glanced down at the images on my desk and saw the feet of a couple walking in the park. Autumn leaves raining around them, but you could only see their legs and some glistening trees in the background. Romance painted so simply. Kind of made me reconsider the blind date idea.

Second one, a man and woman sitting at a piano. Her head on his shoulder and eyes on the keys, while he looked down at her as he played. Very sweet. They both wore all white, a perfect complement to the antique piano. Then I saw the shoes. Those Converse shoes again, barely tied under the piano bench.

I analyzed the art for a few more minutes. Could that really be him? Is he with someone else?

I'm crazy, I thought, then moved on to the next picture and dropped it into my lap. I blinked a few times to make sure. Yes, definitely Sarah looking back at me.

Sarah?

Yes. Sarah. On a park bench under the streetlight. Half moon hanging in the indigo sky behind her. Frost-laden tree branches sparkling in the moonlight, just like her hair and eyes. Angelic and beautiful, she leaned forward on the bench, arms at her sides. I loved the soft brush strokes. His style made every picture look so poetic.

SARAH CAME IN LATE EVERY NIGHT. I DIDN'T SEE HER FOR three days, which wasn't normal since we lived together.

Finally, I stayed up and waited for her to come in. Guess I can't say I actually stayed up. I fell asleep on the couch and woke to the sound of the key turning in the door.

She jumped. "What are you doing awake?"

"What are you doing? I haven't seen you in days."

"I've had a lot going on. Been trying to deal with everything. Not sure what to do."

"Do you want to talk about it?"

Her keys jingled as they landed on the couch beside her. I sat up and pulled the blanket to my chest. She yanked another blanket from the back of the couch and curled up underneath.

The ticking of the clock talked for us. Minutes passed. And a few more. We listened to each other breathe. Her chest rose and fell in a slow rhythm, then she stopped breathing for a second and wiped her eyes.

"Sarah, what's going on? You're worrying me. Is he abusing you?"

"No, not at all. He's fine and supportive and for some odd reason loves me more than I could ever love someone after knowing them for three minutes."

"Three minutes?"

She laughed and sniffed. "You know what I mean."

"Then what is it, Sarah?" I took her hand in mine. "I'm serious. What's wrong?"

"I can't say yet. I'm sorry. You deserve to know everything about my life. You've been the closest person to me for years."

"Then why can't you tell me? I haven't seen you in days, you've been crying yourself to sleep. I even called your parents and they said they haven't been able to get in touch with you either."

"You called my parents?"

"I've never seen you like this. What happened to the joy that never dies? The smile of yours that would sometimes haunt me in my dreams."

She tried not to smile. "It has nothing to do with James. It has nothing to do with anyone but myself."

"Then why can't you tell me?"

She pushed my shoulder. "You're so stubborn."

"You can't always handle things on your own. Sometimes help is needed. There's nothing wrong with that."

She inhaled. Her chest rising and falling to the ticking of the clock. I listened to her cry, then sob into her blanket. In all of my years with her, I never, ever saw her act like that. Of course, my brain went to the worst.

She's been abused, I imagined. She's been raped, something horrible happened. Of course, in all of my twisted thoughts, I never imagined what she'd say next. Too bad Google didn't have a self-diagnosis option for crying best friends.

Again, she dried her face with her blanket and looked at me.

I nodded, reassuring her that I'd listen without trying to talk.

Her lip quivered along with her hands. "I think I have cervical cancer."

Had I been standing, I would have fell to the nearest flat surface. Images rushed through my mind. Chemo, clumps of hair in our bathtub, me losing my best friend, the one who understood me, the only one who could be my maid-of-honor.

"How serious is it?" I managed to whisper.

"I don't know yet. I've never been so scared in my life, Ella." Strands of hair clung to her wet cheeks. "We're so young. I'm not married. There's a chance this is nothing, but my pap-smear came back abnormal. I'm scheduled to have a procedure done once my period is over. That's when I'll know for sure, but Ella, I've looked this up online like crazy and it's got me so worried. It could be nothing, but if it's cervical cancer and it's too late, what next? Not to mention"—she closed her eyes—"what if I lose my chance of having children?"

"I can't imagine going through this. It's hard enough watching this happen to you, but let's not jump to conclusions."

A laugh barely escaped her lips. "Look who's talking."

"I know. Ironic, huh? Seriously though. You are the one who is supposed to think positively. It really could be a fluke, and if it is cancer in the early stages I'm sure everything will be find and you'll be able to have children."

"Will you do me a favor?"

"Anything."

"Promise?"

"Of course. Anything. Really."

"This has my head spinning, not to mention my heart. I'm processing things I never wanted to process this soon. All this to say, part of me wants to marry James just because I wonder who's gonna want me if I can't have kids. Part of me wants to stay single forever because I can't imagine making any man go through that with me."

"I understand, but listen, you really don't know what tomorrow holds. Everything could be fine. Don't think too much about it until you know for sure, okay?"

"Starting to feel like you. How do you think this much on a daily basis?"

"It seems like I do, but I really don't. There's a lot that I question, a lot I wonder about, but I really don't sit around thinking all day about my past or future. I have hope and I live there, in the hope of tomorrow. Sometimes I question myself and that's probably when I seem so out of it, but it's not every day."

"Sure seems like it."

"Lately it has been, but don't compare yourself to crazy people like me. You are my happy sunshine friend. Don't let something like this take that away from you. If you die, die happy. If you live, live happy."

"Wow. What wisdom you have tonight, my dear."

"Yeah. If only I could live by my own words, I'd be a lot better off. So, what is the favor you want from me?"

"I know this will be hard for you, but can we not talk about love and romance for a few weeks? I need a little time to think about life right now without worrying about my love life, and your idealism might make me completely lose my mind right now."

I laughed. "Here's to being honest."

IT MAY BE HARD TO BELIEVE, BUT WITH SARAH'S CANCER scare, I completely forgot about the painting, the Converse shoes, the love of my life waiting in the shadows of who knows where. She asked me to come with her to her procedure. I did. Days later we were watching Kevin Spacey fool everyone in *The Usual Suspects* when Sarah's phone rang.

I listened. Waited. Wondered who called.

Her phone fell to the ground, along with her body.

I picked up the phone. "Hello?"

"Sarah?"

"No, this is her friend. Who is this?"

"This is Dr. Wharton. Please have Sarah call me back tomorrow to set up an appointment. We'll need to go over some things."

"Okay."

"Thank you."

I don't remember if I said goodbye. Sarah, on our living room floor in fetal position, took me to another world. A world I didn't want to be in. Young, like she said. How could this be? Why Sarah? Why not me?

I sprawled out on the floor next to her, head against hers. Sometimes sound isn't needed to express pain. Sometimes the most painful cries are the ones no one can hear. The noiseless whimpers that we hold inside. Maybe we're too afraid of what people think of us. Maybe we are too afraid to let the pain out because we don't want to admit it's there. Maybe we're afraid to start because we'll never stop. Whatever the reason, Sarah didn't cry aloud. Her body, still and warm, occasionally stopped breathing. We stayed there for hours. I pretended to sleep while she pretended not to cry. Minutes ticked by, turning the night into a new day, a new page of life to scribble on. We barely slept. Her, too afraid to close her eyes. Me, too afraid to not be there if she let loose. She never did. We remained there, on the living room floor, as the outdoor lights and sounds lulled us and her silent sobs escorted us to sleep.

We woke up the next morning, early, still on the floor.

"What am I going to do?" Sarah said before most of the city rose for another day of life, another day of life without thinking about death.

I turned to my side and looked at her. "It will be okay."

"This is surreal."

"It is."

The quiet morning soothed our thoughts. Birds sang to us from somewhere outside the window. So many moments in our friendship were filled with that comfortable silence only close friends share. This time, I wished for the words to say. The silence knifed through my heart and chopped it into pieces, so many pieces that I couldn't put it back together to find the words to say.

I guess there are some moments in life that don't deserve the spoken word. Actions are louder and deeper than words could ever be. So, I stayed there with her, in the muted living room, until she finally stood.

"I'm feeling better now," she said. "Thank you for being you."

I stood and hugged her. "I'm here. I know you well. You will survive this with a smile. You're the only person I know who could smile your way to the grave if that's what it came to. This is just the initial shock."

"You're right. I am not going to let this break me. I'm going to smile."

And with that, we smiled our way to the kitchen.

# Ch. 14 | Matthew

The week passed and no, I didn't agree to another blind date. I did spend more time with Heidi, though. We finished the living room and dining room and started priming the master bedroom. Not the most pleasant situation in the world, but the bedroom obviously meant more to her than any other room. She didn't talk much as we primed the walls. She didn't spend much time in the room with me at all, actually. I think it made her too emotional and she didn't want to cry in front of me.

Thankfully, I couldn't make it back until Tuesday, when Gavin decided to come with me. At least I wouldn't be alone as we splashed the primed walls with streaks of crushed berry and charcoal.

She never explained the crushed berry and charcoal colors to me. I didn't expect her to.

Gavin and I stopped in *Chances* on the way to Heidi's. Iced coffees were becoming a must-have for my morning start-up routine. Gavin ordered a hot coffee on a humid August day. Never understood that. Dee helped us. We got to know her pretty well. Nice girl. Funny, she asked me if I'd be willing to go on a blind date with the owner.

"Would that mean I get more of my art in here by default?" Gavin said.

She smiled and gave him his coffee. "I would think so. Especially if it's of Mateo here."

'Blind-dates aren't my thing." I sipped my coffee and looked around. "Look, one of your paintings is already up."

Gavin spun around. "Ah, the one of you and Lydia."

"Is that you?" Dee asked.

I nodded.

"Is that your girlfriend?"

Gavin nodded.

"We just broke up after a very long relationship," I said.

"What happened?" She covered her mouth. "Am I saying too much? Please tell me to shut up if I say too much. I have a tendency—"

"No, it's fine," Gavin said. "Matt here is doing a little soul-searching. He'll figure it all out soon enough. Is the owner here, by the way? I'd really like to thank her for giving me a chance."

Coffee went down the wrong hole. I tried to cough without spraying them and ended up coloring my shirt caramel.

"You alright, man?" Gavin hit my back.

The bells on the door turned our attention to a middle-aged business woman. Gavin and I stepped away from the counter.

"We'll talk to you soon, Dee," Gavin said. "Tell the owner I really appreciate it."

We walked outside and got into my truck.

"What happened with the coffee in there?" Gavin said as I pulled off and stopped at a red light.

"I don't know. It's not like I did it on purpose."

He leaned on the window and looked ahead. "So, you think you'll go on a date with the owner of *Chances*? What are the chances that she is the woman of your dreams?"

"Funny."

"I'm serious. Why not? Kinda weird that Dee asked you and not both of us, isn't it? Maybe it's a sign."

"Not interested."

"Why not?"

"Number one, she's a business woman. Number two, she sounds snobby. Number three, she has classy taste." He pointed at his newly stained and not-so-classy t-shirt. "Number four, I hate blind dates. Number—"

"Alright, alright. How many numbers do you have?"

"A lot. Point being: I'm not interested."

A few songs later and we ended up at Heidi's house. Gavin helped me carry some supplies to the door, but most of it I left at her house since I'd planned on coming back so much.

My knuckles barely reached the door when she yanked the door open and screamed so loud Gavin and I both jumped back. I don't know about him, but my heart flew back to the truck.

She bent over, holding her stomach and laughing. "That was a good one."

Gavin looked at me. I looked at him.

"You feeling okay today, Heidi?" I laughed.

Gavin finally caught on. "Well, nice to meet you, too."

"You must be Gavin." She held out her hand, holding back more laughter. "I've heard much about you."

They shook hands as we entered the house. So glad he didn't say, "Likewise."

Heidi led us to the bedroom and we got our stuff ready right away. Gavin helped me out sometimes so he knew the drill. We worked in silence for a few minutes until Heidi started up the iPod.

"How long have you two been friends?" She sat on the floor and crossed her legs.

Gavin looked at me. "Too long."

"You guys seem pretty close."

"We've been best friends since tenth grade," I said as I focused on painting. "Gavin and I are polar opposites in a lot of ways, but the same in others. I paint on walls, he paints on canvas. We both like coffee, but he likes it hot and I like it cold. We're both passionate and extreme in some ways, but he's more consistent and stable, whereas I fluctuate depending on every factor imaginable."

"He's not lying." Gavin laughed. "The guy could be laughing and happy one minute, the next he's playing depressing songs on the piano and won't talk to you no matter how much you pry him."

"At least I am pry-able, oh mysterious one."

Heidi put her arms behind her back and leaned back. "So how did you guys meet?"

"We went to separate high schools," I said. "But Gavin was dating a girl at my school and ended up at my homecoming dance. And, well . . . ."

Gavin smiled. "Mine as well spill it all."

"Both of our dates ended up dancing with the cooler guys all night long. I guess you could say we were destined to be friends."

Her eyes lit up. "That is hilarious. And you guys were together ever since?"

"Yeah," Gavin continued our story, "and we helped each other through many failing relationships, which, now that I think of it, all had to do with girls ditching us for someone else."

"Sounds harsh," she said . "Guess that's what happens to the nice guys, huh? They always say nice guys finish last."

Gavin stopped painting and looked at Heidi. "Who are 'they' anyway? That's what I'd like to know. Why did they have to say anything at all?"

We all laughed. Gavin and I continued painting. Heidi watched, thinking about Andy I'm sure. So thankful for Gavin's presence in the room. The silence didn't seem awkward. We just listened to music and painted to the melodies. Minutes added up to an hour and Gavin tapped my shoulder.

I looked behind me. At him. Then her.

She dried her cheeks with her sleeve and caught my gaze.

"I'm sorry," she said. "It's this song. And this room."

Not sure I wanted to know why Weezer's *Buddy Holly* had a link to her husband in the bedroom, but I can't say it didn't peak my curiosity.

"You okay?" I said instead.

"Thank you guys for doing this. I really appreciate it."

Gavin and I put our rollers down and sat against an unpainted wall a few feet from her.

One leg up, one leg extended straight, back against the wall, arm resting on knee, Gavin waited a few minutes, knowing I didn't know how to handle these situations like he did. He could draw the heart out of people like their wells never ran dry. I'd spend hours pulling up buckets and leave with nothing, unless they wanted to offer some for free. He always made people feel better. I tended to remain speechless. He's the hugger. I'm the listener. Both are nice, but sometimes people just need a hug and I'm a little awkward in the physical affection area.

He reached forward and turned off the music. "Heidi, do you mind if I ask you a personal question?"

She shook her head.

"What do you think life is?"

She fixed her eyes on the bay window ahead of us, inhaled deeply, then tried to speak. Nothing came out. She shook her head.

"I guess what I'm asking is, what is the purpose of your life?"

"I don't know," she said. "You caught me off guard because for so long my life wrapped itself around Andy's heart and I haven't thought of life outside of him. I'm not sure if I want to."

"I can understand that," I said.

"I can, too," Gavin added. "But I tell this to Matt a lot, and I'll say it to you as well. When we wrap our lives around people or circumstances they will crumble. Matt's life is like a roller-coaster because it is based on the things around him, not the things inside of him."

"Don't worry, Heidi, he tells me this all the time."

"No, no. It's good. Keep going."

"I know you love Andy and always will, and trust me, I can't tell you how much I admire that your ring is still firmly planted on your left hand with no desire to be planted anywhere else."

She twirled the ring on her finger as she focused on Gavin's words.

He pulled his knees to his chest. "I really admire that. I'd never tell you to change that or move on. I'm sure you hear that enough. What I would tell you is to continue to live your life. Your baby needs you to live. And I know Andy would want you to show your child his life by living it for him. You aren't just Heidi anymore, when you married him you became one person."

"I know what you mean," she said. "I guess that's why it's so hard for me to stop crying. A piece of me, literally, is gone."

"It is, but Andy is alive to you. That's something you've made clear. Why not continue living his life through your own? Obviously you can't be him, but part of marriage is growing into better people. The years you would have spent together would have been challenging because they would have taught you to grow in areas you are weak and Andy is strong. There's no reason you have to stop that just because he is gone. Become more like him. Write down his good qualities, the one's that are opposite of yours. And spend your life growing in those areas."

"Well, one thing is for sure." She smiled. "Andy would not be sitting on the floor crying to the painters."

# Ch. 15 | Ella

Waiting for Sarah to come out of the doctor's office and tell me the news couldn't have felt longer. Music didn't even help. Only made me feel worse. So I resorted to silence. Lots and lots of silence. Thoughts bounced back and forth, back and forth, creating enough noise in my brain to make up for the lack of music in my car. I leaned back in the driver's seat and closed my eyes. My own life flashed in still images on the back of my eyelids, taunting me with the past, teasing me with the anticipated future.

I didn't want my life to be like this. I expected to play the violin for the rest of my life, serenading my groom on our wedding day. Since that day, that haphazard so-typical-of-Ella day, my life hasn't been the same. Carefree and unplanned, I was the type of girl who drove hours at random just to see the sunset dye the Chesapeake Bay pink and orange. My parents told me to calm down more times than I can count. Sarah, believe it or not, told me to get serious or I'd never make it anywhere in life. It's not like I was a party girl. I didn't stay out late and I didn't break the rules, or at least not often. I valued this part of my personality so much. Until it completely ruined the one thing I worked my entire life for.

Being a disorganized packer I always waited until the last minute. I had one hour to make it to the airport, not far from me. Plenty of time, I told myself.

The images still haunted me. If I would've done one thing different, just one thing, my entire life would be a different story right now. I'd be on a different chapter, in a different plot, in a different setting. The characters would be different, the pages would be interesting, everything would be the way it was supposed to be.

But it's not.

Sarah tapped on the passengers side window, pausing my journey into the past. I unlocked the door.

She sat down, hands in her lap.

I waited.

She beamed. Ear to ear.

"Good news?"

"I told you I'm not going to let this get me down."

"What happened?"

"It's called a cone biopsy. They'll try that first, it may be enough. If not, I won't be able to have children."

"You're smiling?" My heart quickened. "Does this mean you have cancer?"

She nodded. "I'm smiling because you told me to. Don't tell me not to."

"It's okay to react to this, Sarah. You are only human. I am too. This scares me."

"Honestly, he made me feel a lot better in there today. He explained it all to me and he's pretty certain that this will be all better. I know it's depressing to think of my future without pregnancy and labor, but it will be okay. At least I'm alive. At least I'm here. I have a chance. What worried me before was the unknown. What if I went in there and he told me it's too late? What if he gave me a few months or weeks to live?"

"I know. I can't even imagine hearing those words, especially this young."

"That's what scared me the most. This seems curable. It seems promising. For now, I'm going to enjoy my life and not think about tomorrow, because fact is we could die any moment."

Images flickered in my mind like an old film. The car accident. His lifeless body. My broken heart.

"You're right," I said. "I need to heed that wisdom too."

WEEKS PASSED. I TOOK CARE OF SARAH AND SHE TOOK CARE of me in another way. Her spirit drove nails into my self-pity. At first I thought she faked her joy and smiled because I said she should, but the more time passed the more I realized she couldn't possibly be faking it. She got scared, like any normal person would. She cried, she worried, then she smiled and hasn't stopped since.

I picked up my purse from the dining room table and called to her, "Smells like you're cooking something good, huh?"

"Too bad you have to work. I'm making southwest breakfast burritos, all organic and local produce."

"Save one for me. I'll be back for lunch."

As I walked to my car I thought of her new adventures. All organic, no meat. All natural cleaning products and no more makeup and hair stuff. She researched a lot and believed cancer would go away if she got rid of the toxins and ate better. I hoped so.

Living with her, I decided to change the way I ate and lived too. We both decided to give up makeup, which neither of us wore much of anyway. We made our own deodorant, shampoo, cleaning products, and pretty much anything else you can think of from toothpaste to conditioner. I'm amazed at how many uses coconut oil can have. I noticed a difference in my own health and hoped she would too. Cancer is not something I ever wanted to see my best friend go through, especially not so young.

The few positive things I can say that had come from that experience is that Sarah started trying new adventures, we both got healthier, and I almost immediately stopped living in the past and hoping for the future.

Together, Sarah and I decided to live for today. I reminded myself this as I walked to work. The sound of locusts, the brink of autumn, everything made me feel good. Peaceful. At rest. I just hoped it would last.

I unlocked the door of the cafe and turned the sign to "Open," then meandered around and looked at the art on the walls. I loved my little cafe. Never in a million years would I have imagined myself as the owner of anything. I thought for sure I'd end up playing violin my entire life, traveling the world in great symphonies, doing something that involved the art I so loved, something other than selling it on the walls of *Chances*.

Yet, chance gave birth to *Chances* and the only option I had was to accept it and give it all I could.

I walked behind the counter and organized a few things, turned everything on, refilled the receipt paper for the cash register, and handled a few other things before customers would pour in for a good morning treat. I looked up and noticed a man at the front window. He looked away. Something about him looked familiar, but I couldn't place it. He looked back up. I looked away.

One of those awkward moments. He was actually attractive. If only I could bring myself to make eye contact with him, I thought. When I looked back he was gone. Not meant to be, I guess.

I walked to the front door and caught a glimpse of him before he turned the corner across the street. Converse shoes. Barely tied. My heart raced.

Could it be him?

The him?

I opened the door and realized the sign was turned to closed. How did I manage that?

Someone tapped my shoulder. I jumped and turned around.

"Scare ya?" Dee said, huge smile stretching her cheeks to her ears. "What are you doing out here?"

"I think I saw the Converse shoes guy. Does he have blondish hair?"

"Yep, that's him alright. He normally comes in right as we open. Says he has some job with a widow or something and he's been going every day for the last few days or weeks, I can't remember." She took a breath. "Did he come in?"

"No. We just made eye contact. I had the closed sign up without realizing it."

"Interesting. Did he look like Mr. Right?"

"Maybe. I can't remember details. That night went so fast it feels like a blur in my memory, but crystal clear all at once. I remember his shoes. Yes, they matched the shoes that guy was wearing, but who wears the same shoes for a decade? The guy I saw today had blonde hair. I don't remember his hair color because he had a hat on that night. I remember his eyes, but to be honest, I don't remember them well enough. I just feel like when I see him I will know, and I didn't know when I saw this guy."

"Well, how do you imagine you will know for sure?"

"I guess I assume he will remember me, we'll look at each other across the room, and everything will fall into place like a magical movie scene."

She laughed. "Are you serious?"

I smiled and opened the door of *Chances*. "Only forty-percent."

"What do you really think will happen?"

I walked inside and behind the counter. Dee followed.

"I'm going to make myself a coffee," she said. "Want some?"

"Sure. I'm going to go back to the office now and go through my daily phone calls. Let me know if you need anything."

"I will." She turned toward the coffee machine. "And I didn't forget about my question, but I know you have no idea so you can answer me when you do."

I smiled and walked to my little nook in the back of the cafe. Dee thought she knew me so well, and she did in many ways. We spent most days together. But she never knew me well enough to figure out what my silent moments meant. Sarah could figure me out most of the time. Other than her, people always misread my hushed responses. I liked that. And I couldn't wait for the right man to come along. The man who would be able to read me as though I'm literally a part of him. Because I would be a part of him.

I sat down in my chair and looked at the stack of papers in front of me, then pictured myself feeding my kids chocolate chip pancakes instead of sitting in an office. It didn't make sense. All of this life stuff. Most of my friends found the man of their dreams and started a family shortly after. The man of their dreams. I don't have enough fingers to count the amount of weddings I've been to in my short life. Teary-eyed joyful weddings. Some have been happily-ever-after, some not so much, but either way they found someone to spend their lives with, for better or worse. Sarah's health concerns definitely helped me find contentment, but every now and then when I sat in front of these papers, at this same old desk, I couldn't help but wonder how much longer I needed to wait to find the man for me. Would I find him?

I guess that's the bigger question. Does he exist? Is he a fantasy? Are my expectations too high?

Dee came in and set a steamy cup on my desk. "What's going on in your mind? You look deep in thought."

"Oh, I don't know Dee. Just seems like an eternity when you're waiting for the one thing you've always wanted. Remember what Christmas Eve was like as a kid? That complete anticipation of what was to come. You knew you were going to get gifts, but what would they be? Would you get what you wanted? You could barely sleep, barely dream, just toss and turn and stare at the window until a ray of sunshine told you it was morning." I sipped my coffee and waited for her reaction. She didn't have one, so I continued with my rant. "I guess I feel like that, only more intense. I want to open the gift already, but at the same time I wonder if the gift will be anything like what I wanted. And if it's not, will I be happy with it anyway?"

She sipped her coffee. The bells rang in the front of the shop. I nodded and she walked out to greet the customer. Maybe I didn't want to hear her response anyway. I knew it was selfish of me to think that way even as a child. Why didn't I care more about giving presents? I always wanted to receive them and when I didn't get everything I wanted I actually got depressed. So depressed that I couldn't enjoy the few gifts I did want, because I didn't receive every single gift on my list. Yes, Dee would have definitely reminded me of this. She seemed like a tough girl on the outside. Many people had mistaken her for a self-centered person because of her appearance. She did spend a lot of money on her punk rocker style, but underneath she cared more about others. She always helped others. Went completely out of her way, and like most people besides me . . . she just lived without wishing for things she didn't have.

Eh, she's younger, I'd tell myself. Wait until she's thirty and still single.

Yes, I responded to myself, but you made this choice.

Sarah's smile lit up my thoughts. So much more to life than this nonsense. I really needed to stop thinking about marriage so much.

Dee entered the room again. "So?"

"What?"

"Ready?"

I blinked a few times. "Ready?"

"There's a man out here who would like to see you."

"Are you kidding me?" I motioned for her to close the door. "What are you doing?"

"I'm not doing anything. There's a man out here who asked to see you."

"What kind of man?"

"Would you just go see him?"

I looked around the room, unable to feel my own body anymore. "Is it the Converse guy?"

"Go look for yourself."

"I can't."

"Ella. Seriously. Get up out of your chair and go meet the guy."

I managed to get out of my chair and walk toward the door. "What are you up to?"

"Nothing."

Her smile made me feel uncomfortable.

I peered around the door frame and laughed. "You are horrible, Dee."

I greeted the UPS driver, signed my name, and accepted the rather enormous package.

"Now, tell me this," Dee said. "If you are truly ready for Christmas morning, wouldn't you run down the stairs and open the presents with excitement?"

I nodded. "You are too much."

"Well, wouldn't you?"

"It's different. I'm shy. Meeting men has never been easy for me. Why do you think I'm in this position?"

"You're in this position because you want to be. You've chosen *the one* over *just anyone* and that's what has made you most content. It's only when you start comparing yourself to other people that you lose your marbles."

I set the package down on the floor in my office. "I don't really compare myself. I do wonder how everyone around me has found love, but I can't seem to find it. You are right, though. I'm choosing the one over just anyone and I believe he does exist. Some days my mind gets foggy. I feel like I'm getting old."

"You're going to be thirty, not ninety. You have plenty of life ahead of you."

"Yeah." I cut the tape off the box and opened the flaps. "Wonder what this is."

Bells rang from the front door and Dee disappeared. I managed to find my way through the protective shipping wrappers and a familiar shape caught my attention. Who would send me this? I gently pulled out the beautiful, antique violin and ran my fingers down the strings. Seemed to be in great condition, probably could play beautifully right out of the box. I searched for a card or a receipt, but saw nothing else in the box besides the bow and the violin it belonged to.

# Ch. 16 | Matthew

On my way to Heidi's house I stopped by *Chances* again, but the sign said they were closed. I looked at my watch and peered inside. A pretty woman stood inside, doing something behind the counter. She looked at me, then away. I looked at the sign again and considered waiting, if anything I wanted to introduce myself to the girl inside. We made eye contact again, but she looked away and continued setting stuff up behind the counter. Definitely a pretty girl, but I had to get back to the truck before I got a parking ticket. I parked by a meter without any coins to buy me some time. I figured I'd be quick, but it didn't look like she planned on opening the door anytime soon.

I looked at her one last time and jogged back to my truck. I know it's not right that I enjoyed spending so much time with Heidi, but I did. Maybe it was innocent. I don't know. What I do know is that I loved being with her. Something about her made me want to be better, live better.

As I drove to Heidi's house I imagined Lydia curled up on my bed with one of her favorite books. Feet poking out of the bottom of the sheets because she always felt hot. You'd never know it though. If you touched her skin you would mistake it for an ice cube. The way she looked at me when I'd walk into the room. Always inviting me to come snuggle up beside her with that cute look in her eyes. I loved her. I knew I did. But that's just it. For the last few months I knew that I did love her, but I couldn't figure out if that still lived in the present tense. *Did* needed to stay *do*, and I wasn't so sure anymore.

I pulled up to Heidi's house and before I knew it we were finishing up the paint in her bedroom. She didn't say much this time. Neither did I. We painted as music filled the gaps of our brief conversations until she broke the silence.

"I wanted this room to be these colors because it reminds me of his body the last time I saw him." She wiped her face. "Blood on pavement. Crimson and grey."

I can only imagine how high my eyebrows lifted just then.

"It's not just that," she smiled. "It's also the colors from our honeymoon night. The floor was a grey just like this and he had berry colored rose petals all over the place."

I tried not to imagine the scene.

"I don't ever want to forget seeing his lifeless body because it reminds me of that first night we spent as a married couple, full of life. Both his death and his life. I want them to go hand-in-hand. I want to remember them together. I can't live as though he's still here, but I also can't live as though he's gone. Besides you, I never want another man in this room. Ever."

"Wow." I continued to paint the room, not making eye contact with her. "Gavin is very idealistic and I am too, but you and him have this steady nature that I just can't wrap my head around."

"What do you mean?"

"Well, for starters, my idealism is a true hopeless romantic. Key word, hopeless. I tend to set my standards above reality and hope for things that are hopeless. You and Gavin have hopes, but your idealism doesn't send you flying to the moon. Maybe sometimes Gavin gets the tip of his head in the clouds, but he's never far from the ground. I have no idea how you guys balance your extreme idealistic views with such temperance."

She sniffed and laughed a little. "No one has ever said that to me. Most people just think I'm crazy."

"Maybe you are, but compared to me you are pretty grounded and sane."

"You don't seem as bad as you make yourself sound."

"Ask Gavin. He lives with me. He knows."

She laughed again. "I don't feel very grounded."

"Maybe that's the wrong word. I just mean you guys make a decision, as crazy as it may be, and you stick to it with joy and passion. I can't say I don't envy that."

"So you're saying you are indecisive?"

"Yes. A crazy, passionate, hopeless indecisive person with no direction."

"I don't think so. You have your own business, which seems pretty successful. From what I hear you are a great musician with a lot of talent. You have direction."

"In those things." I finished the last stroke of paint and placed the roller down on the drop cloth. "Not in love."

"Tell me more about Lydia. You've mentioned her several times, but you don't go beyond mentioning."

I rubbed my chin and looked at Heidi's curious eyes.

"It's okay if you don't want to."

"No. It's not that I don't want to. It's that I have no idea what to say because I have no idea what I feel."

"Are you dating other people right now?"

I picked up a few things and sealed the paint cans, then looked at Heidi again. Arms crossed, slight smirk, something Lydia has done so many times in her playful little way.

"I'm open to it," I said. "Gavin wants to set me up on blind dates, but he's done that once and it was a total disaster. Not sure I want to try that again."

"Are you hoping to find someone better?"

"Not at all." I wiped my hands on my jeans. "I don't think of women in that way."

"What way?'

"I don't rate them on scales. No woman is better than another. Without the wild daisy the rose wouldn't seem so elegant. They all have their place in the garden, just not sure which garden I want to plant myself in."

"What if you don't have to worry about that?"

"Huh?"

"I mean, what if where you are planted is exactly where your wife is planted, but you don't know it yet?"

"Right. That's just it. How do you know it? When do you know it? Is Lydia mine or is it someone else?"

"In my opinion, if you don't know it, then it's not right." She shook her hair out of her pony tail and swooped it all back up again. "When it's the one, you know."

"What if there isn't a one? What if I'm just supposed to choose? And what if Lydia never comes back to me, can't blame her if she doesn't, and no one else comes along? What if I'm single for the rest of my life because I didn't take the one option I had?"

"That doesn't sound romantic for someone who considers himself a hopeless romantic."

"Okay." I laughed. "Maybe I'm just hopeless."

I DON'T EVEN KNOW WHY I AGREED, BUT I DID. GAVIN LAUGHED as I walked out the door to pick up his choice for my second blind date and pending calamity.

"It will be fine," Gavin said as I shut the apartment door.

Right, I thought as I jogged down the stairs. He didn't even get to know these girls. He just shipped them my way for testing. At least the last one walked out on me. That made it easy. Last thing I wanted was to break another girl's heart. I still couldn't get Lydia's face out of my head that last time I saw her. Sometimes I'd pick up my phone to text her and ask how she's doing, then I'd stop myself. I knew I'd only bring her more pain. She probably had my number blocked anyway. I'm sure lines of nice guys were waiting at her door for a chance with her.

She deserved better than me.

I got in my truck, hit play on my iPod, and a few songs later I arrived at my date's house. Hopelessly unromantic. I didn't even feel nervous this time, just got out of the truck, walked to the door, and assumed a crazy lunatic would open the door to greet me in a few minutes, take one look at my paint-stained jeans, and walk back inside.

No, I didn't even change my clothes this time. No need to impress anyone. I wanted to be myself. And right now myself didn't feel like trying or caring.

I knocked on the door of a small suburban house.

Waited.

Another minute.

Rang the doorbell and knocked again.

A few seconds later the doorknob jiggled and a beautiful face smiled at me. Wait a second. Beautiful doesn't do it justice. This girl looked like she belonged with on a Calvin Klein billboard, not around my arm.

"You must be Matthew?" she said, eyes sparkling in the setting sun.

I nodded. "And you must be Olivia."

Pretty sure that was the first time my voice cracked since tenth grade science class when Britney Morris sat next to me and asked to borrow my pencil eraser. That was the last she spoke to me and I imagined my date with princess Olivia wouldn't go too far either. Leagues above me. Leagues. What was Gavin thinking? And why didn't he go on a date with this girl? They'd make a better couple for sure.

"Are you okay?" She smoothed her hair behind her ear as I tuned back into my life, wishing I could change the channel.

"Sorry. Long day at work." I fiddled the keys in my hand. "You ready?"

She came outside and stood beside me. Long blonde hair gracing her body well beyond her shoulders. Slender, curvy frame. Simple earrings and makeup. Black flat shoes, blue jeans, and a white tunic hugging her hips and highlighting her neck. Stunningly simple. Beautiful. Out of my league.

I looked at the holes in my jeans. "Sorry I didn't change clothes first."

"What?" Her smile could intoxicate me if I let it. "I kind of like it. Rugged."

"Yeah." I laughed and walked toward my truck. "I guess that's me."

She followed. I opened the passenger's side door and watched her hop into the seat. I'd be a liar if I said I wasn't attracted to this girl, but really, what on earth was Gavin thinking?

I walked around the truck and opened my door. "You aren't a vegan, are you?"

She smiled. "No, vegetarian. Why?"

"Are you going to flip out on me if I eat something that once lived and breathed on this earth? Because if so, you might want to run back inside before it's too late."

I sat down and turned the keys in the ignition.

"Bad blind date experience last time?" she said, big green eyes fixed on me.

"Did he tell you?"

"Maybe." She held back a laugh. "I won't get upset with you for eating the flesh of another living creature, but your body might."

I accelerated the car and looked ahead. "Why do you say that?"

"Well, I'm not a vegan so I do eat animal products, but I'm choosy about which ones. Animal flesh just isn't my friend. If I eat it I feel horrible afterward."

"Well, can't say I have that problem."

"Yet. You might not be saying that when your clogged arteries are being cleared out before you turn fifty."

"So, where do you want to go?"

"Right now?"

I nodded, still looking at the road ahead. What an odd date. I kind of felt bad that I didn't care enough to try to be a charming date. Truth is, I couldn't get Heidi out of my head. Until I remembered her growing stomach with a living person inside of it.

"Is that okay?" Olivia interrupted me.

"Sorry. What did you say?"

"How about we go to the movies?"

I nodded again. "Can you type that into your phone and see where the nearest one is?"

"Sure."

The GPS on her phone directed us to the nearest movie theatre as we talked about normal things like we'd known each other for years. She didn't seem to care about my nonchalant demeanor. If she knew me better she would have realized that I was in a bad mood and didn't really care if I ever saw her again, but I couldn't help but realize how sweet-spirited she was for such a beautiful girl.

That sounds bad. What I mean is that most gorgeous girls I've met seem to be uptight and more concerned about reapplying their lipstick than anything substantial. That's not me. If I were a character in *Lord of the Rings*

I'd for sure be a hobbit. Simple.

I decided to use that as a conversation starter. "If you were a character in *Lord of the Rings*, who do you think you'd be?"

Her sweet smile brightened the car as I opened my door and walked around to her side to open hers.

She took my hand and stepped out. "*Lord of the Rings* is my favorite movie series ever. I watch it once a year."

"Really?" I smiled. "Me too. Gavin is more of a *Braveheart* kind of guy. I sit through that with him and he sits through *Lord of the Rings* with me."

"You guys are so romantic."

We laughed. Our eyes met for a second. A second that made me believe I could possibly allow myself to like her. I looked away and shook the thought.

"Let me guess," I said. "You'd be Arwen?"

"I'm not as predictable as you think." She opened the door of the theatre before I could open it for her. "See."

"Okay, so you like to be a little manly sometimes? In other words, you'd be Eowyn?"

We laughed again. I opened the second door for her and we entered the dimmed theatre.

"I would be Legolas," she said.

"Legolas? Don't you have to pick a woman?"

"You never said I had to be a woman."

"Well, aren't you a woman?"

"Sure I am. Arwen is a nice character. I love her strength and femininity. I love that she fights for her love and would give up her entire life for him. Literally. That's one of the most beautiful scenes. The one where she says she'd rather spend one lifetime with him than a thousand without. I love that so much. Eowyn is a little too fighter-spirited as a woman for me. I don't have that much gusto and don't like the idea of women fighting in wars. But I love the elves. There's something so beautiful and faithful about them. And Legolas, I mean, come on, who is cooler than Legolas?"

"That's funny you say that because he is my favorite character. I'd definitely be Legolas if I had my choice, but I'm probably more like a Samwise in reality."

"Does that make Gavin Frodo?"

"Gavin is Aragorn. No doubt about it. Handsome. Kingly. Passionate, but quiet and reserved."

"You make him sound so appealing."

"I'm surprised you don't think so."

"He's not my type."

I walked up to the cashier. Olivia followed behind and stood close to my arm. Close enough to smell her soft jasmine scent.

"Any ideas on what to watch?" I said.

She shook her head. Delicate pressing into her slightly pink cheeks.

I chose the movie. No romance. No comedy. Just a normal drama flick. Figured middle of the road was the best choice for a first date. After paying for the tickets we walked to the back and found our theatre number.

"So." I opened the door for her. "What is your type?"

She walked in the theatre, leaned back, and whispered in my ear. "Wouldn't you like to know."

# Ch. 17 | Ella

Patrick called me. I wouldn't have accepted his request to get together, except that he sounded as though he'd be crying and he asked me if I'd be willing to meet him at his wife's grave. I figured that didn't sound like an attempt to seduce me, so went ahead and met him there.

As I walked through the graveyard I saw him. Arms dangling at his sides. Shoulders heavy, head down. I approached the grave. And him. He attempted to smile, but failed.

I put my hand on his shoulder. "Are you okay?"

He nodded. "I'm sorry to make you do this. I figured I could consider you a friend and no one else understands."

"Please don't worry. I'm glad you called."

He did a good job holding back tears, except for the slight quiver of his bottom lip.

"Thank you for coming." He never made eye contact with me, only the gravestone in front of us. "Everyone is telling me to move on. Everyone. Maybe it's because I can't get out of my depressed stupor. Maybe they miss seeing me happy."

"You need to find happiness, Patrick. You can't go on living like this. She wouldn't want that."

I looked at the gravestone his gaze still rested on. *Emily May Wheldon. Beloved wife of Patrick. Daughter, sister, and faithful friend.* Our silence, carried by the autumn breeze, made my mind wander off to the color-changing trees. The cycle of life.

"Look over at those trees," I said. "So many beautiful colors and yet they are dying. Do you ever wonder if it's just us? Just our culture that makes us look at death as a negative, sad thing? When really it's this beautiful experience that ends up being the most colorful one of our lives?"

Patrick finally made eye contact with me, then looked back to the trees. "You lost me."

I laughed. "I just mean that Emily's death was probably the best time of her life. The time where she learned the most about how to truly live. When we're faced with death we grow from it in ways we never could've in our normal busy lives. We change. Like the trees. We change into something even more beautiful. Maybe that's what death is. A transformation into true beauty, into real life. And maybe that's what you need to do."

"You mean I need to die too?"

"No." I smiled. "I'm not that deep, am I? I'm just saying you need to embrace Emily's death as something beautiful. Something good that happened to her. And something beautiful that's happened to you because of her. Allow this to change your colors, to help you live a content and captivating life before you die one day yourself."

"Yeah. I guess one thing this has shown me is my own mortality."

I looked at the name on the stone again. Then the others around us. So many stones spanned out for miles and miles. Body after body piled under mounds of earth and grass. The final chapter of every story lied six-feet under. Or did it?

"My friend Sarah recently had a scare with cervical cancer. It's not a big deal now, but it really changed the way we think about life."

He sat on the grass, crossed one leg over the other, and leaned back onto his hands. "How so?"

I sat beside him, indian-style. "It taught us to live, to put it simply. To just be. But at the same time, to care more about our health and not just live for pleasure and enjoyment. To be responsible with each day we're given and not look ahead, wondering why today doesn't look like we hoped it would yesterday."

We looked at each other until I broke eye contact by looking down at my hands, filled with the grass I had picked apart as we talked. The crisp air rustled the leaves by our feet as we allowed the silence to once again fill the space between us. I felt natural with Patrick. In a sense, I wished he weren't a widow. I would've considered giving up my dreams of Mr. Coffee Shop if so. But reality always looked dimmer than my dreams and unfortunately I couldn't turn off the light.

WHEN I WALKED INTO MY APARTMENT THAT NIGHT I SAW A note on the kitchen counter. Sarah let me know that she'd be back tomorrow. Not to worry. No other hints. She knew that would drive me nuts. I tried to call and text her to no avail. Phone turned off.

I am an open book. My Sarah is a locked journal who gives away the key long enough for you to take a peak, but not read anything in detail. Then she closes herself back up and hides the key.

I never understood that personality. What's there to hide? She's also the type to wait three days before making a first date think she's interested. I know her motivations aren't devious, but I can't help but wonder why all the games. If you want something, get it. If you like someone, show it. If you are sad, cry. Happy, smile. No point in hiding things and pretending to be one thing when you're really another.

Honestly, I don't have the energy for that. Enough thoughts pound their fists against my brain cells every day that I can't conjure up the ability to pretend to be something I'm not.

So, here I am.

A few weeks ago I would have called myself depressed. Hopeless, albeit anticipating a better future. Now, not so much. More like hopelessly hopeful and somewhat content.

Let's be honest, I'm not the type to be completely content until all my ducks are neatly clucking one behind the other. Right now, my ducks are frantically trying not to drown in a turbulent river.

Okay, maybe it's not that bad.

My phone rang. I didn't recognize the number, so I let it go to my voicemail. When the little notification popped up I called and listened to the message.

"Hi Ella. I hope you are doing okay. I wanted to call you about something really important that will affect *Chances*. If you could, please return my phone call as soon as you can."

The tone of his voice reminded me of wilting flowers underneath the scorching sun. Not sure I wanted to hear the really important news, but I called back anyway.

"Ella, I'm glad you called. Listen," Mr. Sullivan said. "We've had a bad year with the building and, well, the bills haven't been paid with our current expenses. We haven't been able to find anyone to rent the upper portions of the building and we can't afford to keep it going."

"Okay." I swallowed hard. "What does this mean for me?"

"Well, it means we are selling the place and you can either buy it and stay where you are or hope that the next landlord is willing to allow you to stay there."

"Is that probable?"

"Can't say for sure. Depends what kind of vision they have for the place and if you fit into that vision."

My shop. How could it be taken from me in the blink of an eye? Just like that. I didn't even know this could happen.

"Are you okay?" he asked.

"Sorry. Yes, thank you Mr. Sullivan." I exhaled. "Thank you for telling me. I'll figure something out if it comes to that. We'll see, I guess. I'm sorry to hear things have been rough financially."

"Well, it's okay. We are actually thinking of selling our house too and moving back to Lancaster to be closer to our grandchildren. It's all for the best."

"Yes."

All for the best.

"ARE YOU SERIOUS?" DEE SUNK INTO THE CHAIR ON THE other side of my desk. "What does this mean for *Chances*?"

I shook my head. "No way to know for sure until someone buys the place."

"And you can't afford to buy the building?"

I raised my eyebrows. "The question is, even if I could, would I really want to?"

She looked around the room. "Well, I better start looking for something else in case."

"Of course. That's exactly what I want you to do. How's the savings account for your studio?"

"It's coming, but not quite there yet." She stood. "I want to start it right."

"Yes. I'm supportive of waiting for the right thing."

She rolled her eyes with a slight smirk and then walked out of my office. I looked at the box to my left. Flaps folded over, hiding the instrument inside. Tempting. So tempting to try to play again, but I feared the memories and worse . . . the pain of resurrecting the memory of his dead body.

The front door bells jingled. Dee walked back into my office, sunlight from the doorway highlighting her frizzy hair.

"Looking at that violin again, huh?" she said. "Plan on picking it up anytime soon?"

I shook my head.

"You never told me what happened. Why don't you play anymore?"

"It's a long story."

She looked out the door. "It's 1:45pm on a Tuesday. I have time for a long story."

"Guess I don't have a choice."

She sat down and crossed her legs. "All ears."

"It's really not that big of a deal. I don't like telling people for that reason alone."

"Because you are afraid I will think you are ridiculous?"

"To put it plainly, y—"?

"I already do. No worries there." The bells jingled again. "Bet that's UPS. Be right back."

I heard a customer order a latte as I pulled out some paperwork to go through. Not like I had time to sit around and play violin or talk about why I don't anymore. Mr. Sullivan left a message on my phone. The *for sale* sign would be up in a few days, but he already had a promising buyer. Except they wanted to turn it into a parking garage. He also gave me a few ideas for new locations. Even told me I'd be more successful if I moved the shop.

Trouble is, I liked *Chances* being there. Not only did the business thrive from day one, but I'd have to bury my dreams if I left. Something I had no desire to do. Not yet.

I knew he would come back one day. Whether he thought about me or not, he'd show up in Chances one day purely because he used to work in the same place years ago. I've prepared myself for the possibility of him walking in with his wife's hand linked in his, but I didn't mind. Seeing him one last time would give me the closure I needed to let the dream die.

Patrick's face halted my mental rant. His sad eyes looking for hope in all the wrong places. My grandfather's words. So pure and true. The last words he spoke to me have never left my mind, but somehow they fluttered away from my heart more than I wanted them to.

We didn't expect him to die when they operated on his heart that day. No one did. No one except him.

He squeezed my hand.

"I know you don't like seeing me like this," he said, surrounded by wires and beeping machines.

"I don't at all." I wiped away a single tear.

"Listen to me." The brightness on his face turned dark, serious. "I need you to do something for me."

I leaned in. "Anything."

"Never give up hope until you find whatever it is you are after, but . . . . "

"Yes?"

"Just don't spend your life looking for hope in the wrong places. You'll never find it."

One month and four days later, I left in a hurry for the airport. I had an extremely important audition. Already late, I stopped when a nice guy from my apartment building asked me if I wanted to go out on a date. I had been dreaming of that moment for weeks. I shouldn't have stopped. He only wanted me for one thing and I wasn't about to give him that one thing. I found out the hard way.

Pushing it, my car reached over ninety on the speedometer several times. By the time I got to the Philly bridge I slowed down to eighty. One glance over at the water and my life changed forever. Everything after that is a blur. All I know is I crossed the lines. I hit another vehicle, which turned into a five car accident right in the middle of the bridge. I broke my arm in two places, took months to recover from, and most of all, ruined my ability to play even the most simple scale on my violin.

The doctor said I'd have a full recovery and I believed him, but every time I picked up a violin my hands no longer did what I wanted them to do. But that's not what made me give up. How could I pick up a violin and play when I killed a five-year-old little boy with an entire life ahead of him? Because of me, parents went home to an empty boy's room and probably curled up under Batman sheets in tears. Because of me, Parker Ramsey's body was lowered into the earth as rain pelted his casket and his daddy held his mommy from trying to hysterically jump into the earth with her son. I watched from a distance. Walked away with tear-saturated clothes. I hadn't picked up a violin since. Everyone thought it was because of my injury. That's what I wanted them to believe.

I wanted to hope. I wanted to believe my grandfather's last words. Perseverance paid off my entire life. From Honor Roll to the world renown violinist I could've become. But somehow I allowed that instrument, my voice, to become buried with Parker. In the ground. Dead to this world. Believing that perhaps I needed to look elsewhere for the so-called hope I promised my grandfather I'd never give up.

Problem is . . . I never discovered the right place to look.

# Ch. 18 | Matthew

I liked Olivia. Don't get me wrong. The girl had beauty, brains, and charm. But being with a girl who is eyed up by every man within a one mile radius isn't my idea of fun. I know some guys like the whole trophy wife thing. They want a wife who looks good because they think it makes themselves look better or at least feel better. I have no desire to look or feel better. I know who I am and I'm comfortable with my shoes, beat up as they might be.

High maintenance and I don't go hand-in-hand. In fact, high maintenance will eventually realize that although I can repair just about anything in a house . . . I refuse to repair bruised egos with shiny shoes and two-hundred dollar hair appointments.

I'm a simple guy. And I wanted a simple woman. Simple is romantic to me. Ordering pizza and talking on the couch is more romantic than a fancy dinner and a bottle of wine. That's one reason I loved Lydia. She and I never fought over what to do or what to eat or how to be. And although she could spend a million years on her hair and makeup, she didn't mind if I ruined her curls by running my fingers through her hair. Or if I smudged her makeup when I kissed her eyelids. I loved kissing every centimeter of her sweet face.

"What are you thinking about now?" Gavin walked into the room. "Sounds depressing."

"What's new, right?"

"So I take it your date with Olivia won't be turning into another date?"

I removed my hands from the piano keys in front of me and turned to face Gavin. "Did you have to ask? Do you even know me at all? Why would you think I'd like someone like Olivia?"

"Well, you said you wanted someone different, something else. I'm trying to help you find that."

"I don't want someone different. I love everything about Lydia."

"Then why aren't you with Lydia?"

I turned back to the piano. "It's more complicated than that."

Gavin's footsteps trailed off. "If you say so."

After another moody melody I knocked on Gavin's bedroom door.

"Yeah?" he said.

"Can I come in?"

"Of course."

Gavin's room and my room looked as opposite as him and I did. He could've been a spokesperson for Ikea. Everything Ikea. Spotless and modern. He took care of his stuff. Enter my room and beware of the mountain of clothes piled up on the floor. Right next to the basket they belong in, mind you.

"So what's going on in the mellow yellow world of Matthew?" Gavin put his iPad down and leaned against the black headboard of his bed.

"Just bored." I sat in a chair by his desk. "What's going on in your life oh mysterious one?"

"There is something."

"By the looks of your face it's something good."

"Do you think it's possible to find the girl from the coffee shop years ago?"

"I gave up on that kind of hope long ago. We don't live in a Nicholas Sparks movie and I'm not sure I'd want to."

"But let's say something like that were possible . . . would you want to be with her or would you settle for someone else?"

"I don't know. Why do you have to make my life more complicated than it already is? Isn't that my job anyway?"

He smiled and picked up his iPad.

"Leaving me on that note, huh?"

"Just thinking." He slid his finger across the glossy screen. "Why don't you go play us a song piano man? I'm actually in the mood for depressing for once."

"Funny, because I'm not."

MY PHONE RANG AS HEIDI AND I FINISHED UP THE LAST FEW strokes of the turquoise bathroom. I didn't recognize the number, so I let it go to voicemail, but it rang again.

"You gonna get that?" Heidi said.

I nodded. "Hello, Matt speaking."

"Hey Matt," the familiar voice said. "Know who this is?"

"Forgive me, but I'm not sure I do."

"It's Dee. From the cafe. You didn't stop in this morning."

I laughed. "Am I that regular now?"

"Well, yeah. But hey, I had a question for you and since I had your number I figured why not ask, right?"

"No problem. What do you need?"

"Well, I asked you about going on a blind date with the owner here before, right? Her name is Ella. Not sure if I told you that already or not. Anyway, she said she saw you the other day outside of the cafe. Did you see her?"

"Yes. I didn't realize it was her though. Not as businessy as I thought she'd be. I thought it was just another girl like yourself or something."

"Yes, she's unusual like that. Fine taste in art, but not so much in clothing. Simple gal. Anyway, how about that blind date?"

I paused. Frozen by my fear of letting another girl down. Or letting myself down. Again and again.

"Please?"

"What's in this for you?"

"I just want to see what happens."

"A real live Cupid, huh?"

"You could say that."

"I don't know. I appreciate the thought, and she is pretty, don't get me wrong."

"But. . . ."

"I loathe, absolutely loathe, blind dates."

I caught Heidi's smile and rolled my eyes.

She raised her eyebrows and gave me the eyes, then whispered, "Do it."

"How about I make you a deal?" Dee said.

"And what would that be?"

"I will get one of Gavin's paintings sold, get you a gig in here on our busiest night, and all you have to do is entertain a beautiful woman for an hour Friday night."

"Wow. You've got a deal."

We hung up and Heidi smiled at me.

"So you're going on another blind date, huh?" she said.

"Don't look so excited. Are you and Gavin and Dee ganging up on me or something?"

She smiled and finished washing her hands, then scooted out of the bathroom. I followed her down the hallway, the steps, and into the kitchen. Heidi became a true friend to me, like a sister. I admired her so much and loved our time together. We had one more room left to paint after the bathroom. The baby's room. But I knew we'd stay in touch. And I'm glad because she really needed friends to be near her during this time. We poured some water and sat at the kitchen table.

"I have a confession." She finally broke the comfortable silence between us.

"Yes?"

"There's something I've been thinking about lately and it's really eating at me."

"What is it?"

She tapped her fingers on her legs and looked everywhere but my direction. I allowed the silence to take a seat at the table again, figuring she would escort it away when she wanted.

The clock on the wall ticked. Birds flew from branch to branch in the tree by her kitchen window. We took turns sipping our waters as I waited for her to usher silence away, but she never did.

I pushed my chair back and stood. "Well, I better get going. Now I have to go cry myself to sleep over this future blind date failure."

"Oh stop." She stood beside me and took my empty glass. "It's not that bad. You never know, you may fall head over heels."

I shrugged. "Doubtful."

Heidi swept her hair into a loose bun in the back and caught me staring at her. We both looked away and I headed for the door. She followed. If I closed my eyes I could almost hear *Moonlight Sonata* in her steps. Something in the air. Something different about her demeanor today. Her smile seemed a little dim and her heart a little heavy.

"If you need anything, anything at all." I said as I opened the door and stepped out.

"I know you're there for me."

I walked away from her weak smile and wished she would've opened up to me, but I figured she would when she wanted. Maybe I'm not the right person for that anyway. I found myself constantly wrestling between romantic and sisterly thoughts of her. Until I reminded myself that the reason I loved her the most was her unabashed faithfulness to her husband.

FRIDAY SNUCK UP ON ME QUICKER THAN I HOPED. I OPENED my eyes and looked at the clock beside my bed. Ten in the morning. Most people already started the last day of their work week and then there's me. Still in bed.

The shower water hissed in the background. Gavin had a big art show in Lancaster tonight. First Friday. They do this big thing every first friday of the month. All the art galleries and shops in Lancaster have little freebies and fun events. People walk around and love it. I went one time. Bored me to death, so I haven't been back since. He goes to meet people and sell stuff. Understandable.

I rolled over and meandered to the kitchen, a magnetic force pulling me toward the orange juice. Not looking forward to this blind date.

The shower water stopped and Gavin walked out a few seconds later.

"What are your plans for today?" he said. "Want to come with me to Lancaster? I could use some company."

"Nah. I've got big plans."

"You? Big plans?" He walked into his room.

I stayed in the hallway and leaned against the wall. "I promised Dee from *Chances* that I'd go on a blind date with her friend there, the owner."

"Oh yeah? Decided she isn't too snobby for you after all?"

"I saw her the other day. She looks pretty low key. Who knows. I'm doing it more for everyone else than I am myself."

Gavin got dressed, made a quick breakfast, we talked about random stuff, and he left. The rest of the day went by slow as can be. Dee told me to meet Ella at a nearby park at four. When the clock finally hit three I showered and put on my nicer jeans and a normal black t-shirt. Looked in the mirror a few seconds, laughed at myself, and walked out the door.

It was nice enough outside to walk instead of bothering with the car. So I took shortcuts and alley ways and found myself sitting on a bench in the middle of the park, waiting for another woman to let down. Not that I thought I was better than her. Definitely not. Just that I knew most likely it wouldn't work.

There was always something that kept me from happily ever after. Just wished I knew how to figure that out and get rid of it.

# Ch. 19 | Ella

My heart raced all day. Even kept me from sleeping. I didn't think Dee would actually set me up with Converse shoes, but she did. And I couldn't get him out of my head since. Over and over I played scenarios in my mind and helplessly watched as they took up residence in my fertile heart.

Now, a few minutes before walking out the door to meet him, I wanted to run back inside and call it off. What if it was him? The him? What if he didn't recognize me? What if we didn't like each other?

I didn't want to see my dreams in the trash can. At least when dreams are out of reach they maintain a hope that doesn't surface. But there isn't much hope left underneath when a dream dies.

I walked the streets of Philly to a nearby park. We said we'd meet on a bench in the middle.

Butterflies swirled and fluttered in my stomach. I wiped my palms on my jeans and told myself to breathe. As I rounded the path of the park I saw him. Converse shoes loosely tied. Legs spread. One hand on his left leg, right arm resting on the bench.

He looked familiar, but could it really be him?

I stepped behind a tree and looked closer, squinting to see through the rays of sun in my eyes. He shifted and looked in my direction. I jumped behind the tree. Hand on my chest, I tried not to laugh. How ridiculous of me.

I turned to peek again.

"Ella?"

My eyes stayed down. On his shoes. The same shoes from that long lost day. Same color, same loose laces. No doubt in my mind.

"I'm sorry." I looked into his eyes. Analyzed his face from the messy blonde hair to the stubble on his defined jaw. "I probably look like an insane person. So embarrassing."

He laughed. "It's okay. I have a great love for trees too."

I smiled, still analyzing his face. Still wondering. I couldn't tell. This wasn't how I wanted it to be.

He stared at me. Curiosity lingering in his gaze. I felt like we were swimming around, looking at each other through different glass bowls. Just breathing and waiting.

"You look so familiar," he said.

I came up for air. "You do, too."

"Oh, I know what it is."

My heart dropped.

"You are in those photographs hanging in *Chances*, aren't you?"

My heart dropped again. Not exactly the romantic twist I longed for. "That's me. My friend Sarah is a photographer."

"Sarah?"

I followed him to the bench. "Yeah, she's my roommate. Best friends for a long time."

"I think she knows my roommate. Gavin. He's a painter. He's been friends with this girl for a long time. She does photography and they've been teaching each other a thing or two. I think he has a secret crush on her, but he has never said anything. He holds his feelings inside a lot and I'm not strong enough to yank them out of him."

"I think they are friends. One of the paintings he sent to *Chances* was a beautiful one of her. I completely forgot about that now."

We sat down. On complete opposite sides of the bench.

I smiled.

"What's the smile for?" he said.

"I just think it's funny that we're sitting so far from each other. This isn't the climactic day I thought it would be."

He inched closer. "How's this?"

I laughed.

"What kind of climactic day were you hoping for? I'm sorry to disappoint you. I have a way of doing that with the ladies."

"No, no. It's not you. I guess I've just been living a fantasy life for so long, hoping one day I'd fall in love with Jane Austen passion. I think all this daydreaming is starting to make me feel like a five-year-old twirling around in a fluffy dress."

"Well, if it makes you feel any better, I loathe blind dates like this. How can two people really fall in love with all this pressure? It's just awkward to me. I always wanted to find my love across a coffee shop or on a street corner. Ours eyes would meet and we'd know and the rest would be history."

I looked down and pulled at a loose string in the hem of my shirt. Inside my mind went crazy. This seemed like the him I've been waiting for all of these years. But this definitely didn't play out like I thought it would. In fact, I couldn't even bring myself to ask him if that really was him all those years ago, because obviously he didn't remember or care to remember me all of those years. How could I tell him that I fell in love with him across a coffee shop, but he didn't fall in love with me? He would think I was nuts if I told him I waited for him.

I wanted to go home.

"Have I offended you?" he said. "I can inch even closer if you want."

I smiled. "You are quite the charmer, huh?"

"Indeed, I try."

"Tell me about yourself. Why are you single and why are you sitting here with me?"

"Wow. Loaded questions right off the bat."

"I'm sorry. I tend to do that. Please don't feel pressured to answer them."

"Well, I don't know. We're on a date. Are we supposed to talk about why we are single?"

"If I told you why I was single you would think I'm crazy. Your story can't be nearly as odd."

"Now that's got me intrigued." He stood. "Let's walk this way for a little."

I stood and followed. "Were you in a serious relationship before? There has to be a reason your friends want you to go on blind dates. Dee told me your friend has been trying to set you up with different women for the last few months."

"Yes. It's true."

"And you didn't like them? How many?"

Hands in his pockets, he smiled. "Will this interview be documented?"

"Am I asking too much? Just tell me."

"It's fine. Just funny, that's all. I only went on two dates. The first one was enough to make me never want to do it again and probably sent her to the psych ward. The second was beautiful, but a little too beautiful if you know what I mean. And there's this other girl, but she's a young pregnant widow, and, well, I don't see that working out."

"Sounds like you might want it to?"

"Honestly, I've thought about it. She's pretty, sweet, and funny. But the main reason she stood out to me is the main reason I can't be with her even if I wanted to."

"And what's that?"

"She's been faithful and plans to be faithful to her late husband for the rest of her life. She said no man will ever be worth taking off her ring. It's endearing to see someone so devoted, willing to sacrifice the rest of her life for him. It's amazing to me because most women spend their lives planning their wedding day and living happily ever after with their husband, but her happily ever after died and she has no desire to continue writing the story without him."

"Wow."

We kept walking. Our strides in sync. Our eyes ahead. We left the park and ended up on a street corner. I kept walking and his hand grabbed my arm. A car whipped around the corner, music blaring.

I liked his hand on my arm, but everything about this felt so strange. What kind of bizarre movie did I jump into?

"You want to get something to drink?" he said.

"Sure." I followed his lead. "Just not from my place."

"So, tell me your odd story of singleness."

"Let's just say it's strikingly similar to your friend, except my husband isn't dead."

"You are married?"

"Never been married. Never really had a serious relationship. What about you? What sparked this blind date adventure?"

"I've had two serious relationships. One would've never worked, but it broke my heart nonetheless when she left. The second ended not too long ago."

"Why?"

"I don't know. Maybe because I'm stupid. Maybe my head is in the clouds."

"I've heard that one too many times myself."

"So you're a wee idealistic too, huh?"

"Maybe."

He opened the door to a little coffee house. I slipped inside. He followed and motioned for me to sit by the window.

"I'll go get us something to drink. You save us a spot here."

"Sure."

I sat and waited for him, watching him as he paid. Kindness emanated from him. Physically, no matter how many times I eyed the guy up and down, I couldn't tell for sure if it was the guy I'd been waiting my life to see or not. I needed to ask.

He walked to the table with two iced teas and a plate of snacks.

"So your friend that likes Sarah." I squeezed some lemon into my tea. "How did you two meet?"

"Gavin? Him and I were friends since high school. Both ditched by our dates at a dance and been inseparable ever since. We worked at a coffee shop for a little bit right after high school, then lived in. . . ."

He kept talking, but I didn't hear a thing. My heart stopped and I knew it had to be him, but sadly, I didn't want it to be. This isn't how I wanted the story of my life to be written.

"What about you?" he said.

"What about me?"

"You and Sarah? How did you meet? Is she single, by the way?"

"She's with someone. Unfortunately. Or we could play Cupid ourselves. We met forever ago. Same school, same dreams. Complete opposite in every other way though."

"Sounds like me and Gavin. If he has any trace of idealism in him it's hidden. Sometimes I just want him to spill his heart so I feel a little less crazy, but he rarely does and when he does it always sounds so calm. I can't imagine being so stable."

I laughed. "I know what you mean."

"So you've never been in a serious relationship?"

"I know it sounds unbelievable. I just never gave my heart away. Wanted to save it for the right person."

"How will you know when it's the right person?"

"I am beginning to wonder that myself."

People walked by the window. So many couples. And then me. Sitting with the man I waited my entire life to sit with. The man I passed up many other opportunities for. The man I created *Chances* for, with the hope of finding him and falling in love. I'm sitting here wishing I weren't sitting here with him. Wishing I never missed that flight, never ended up at that coffee shop instead, never got into that car accident, never broke my arm, and never stopped playing my violin.

My choices left me without any choices. At the end of a long road that just got lonelier. Every rational thing someone has said to me over the years crashed into my heart like a tsunami of the reality I never wanted to face. Now I was drowning in it.

They were right.

"Tell me about the relationship you recently ended. What happened? Why did it end?"

"It's a long story. And I honestly don't know if I understand it myself. I guess I wanted to find someone different, experience something else."

"Do you love her?"

"I don't know."

"How can you not know if you love someone?"

"I guess that's just it. I don't know, so maybe I don't."

"How often have you thought of her since you broke up?"

"Constantly."

My heart could handle this. I let him go. The idea of him died when the real him stepped into my life. I could handle this, I kept telling myself.

"Like right now. The way you are twirling your hair around your ring finger. She did that. Everything reminds me of her. You didn't put sugar in your tea. She put two of the little pink packets in hers. I compare every detail of every woman I meet to her, and somehow everyone pales in comparison."

"It sounds to me like you love her. Why aren't you willing to accept that yourself?"

"I don't know. I guess I wanted to fall in love again. Or feel that newness again. Just experience someone different. Someone more like myself."

I laughed. "Like yourself?"

"She loves music, but I play music. She spends hours on her hair, I don't. She works with kids with disabilities, they are so fragile that I clam up around them. We're so different."

"And why is that a bad thing?"

"I guess it's not."

"Can I give you a little bit of advice?"

"Well, I guess that's what blind dates are for, right?"

I smiled. "We're friends now and that's all we'll ever be, because you are going to march right up to this girl and profess your love to her."

"I am?"

"Look, you are so enamored by your friend who stayed faithful to her deceased husband. I can almost guarantee you that this girl of yours—what's her name?"

"Lydia."

"I can almost guarantee you that Lydia is waiting for you right now, the love of her life who is practically dead to her. You, by choice, wanted to die to her. You wanted to try to let her go and find someone else. Fact is, you can't. You're still in love with her. And I will bet you money that if you went to her right now and proposed to her she would whisper yes with tears in her eyes."

"She's probably moved on. I kept her waiting around for too long. I hurt her so many times. There's no way she'd want me now."

"Would you like to bet money on it?"

He laughed and stood. "Let's head back."

"Actually, there's a nice jewelry store on the corner of this block. Let's head there."

"Are you kidding me?" He opened the door for me. "This is about the strangest date I've ever been on."

I laughed. "You love her, Matt. You love her. You love her. You love her."

"I guess I do."

We walked down the street and I caught our reflections in a glass building. Never imagined I'd meet him and send him off to marry someone else. Never imagined my life to end up like this at all. But things were about to change in my life too.

The time had come.

# Ch. 20 | Matthew

It felt like an eternity as I waited for Gavin to come home from Lancaster. I couldn't wait to tell him about my day. When he finally walked through the door I practically jumped on top of him. Okay, not really, but I paced the living room waiting for the door handle to turn.

"Hey. What are you doing?" Gavin said with tired eyes.

"What do you mean?"

"Pacing the living room at two in the morning? I've seen more interesting things I suppose."

"I have something to tell you."

"Oh boy. Blind date with the owner turned into a love story in the amount of time it took me to go to Lancaster and back?"

"Yes, but not what you think." I pointed to the dining room table.

Gavin inched closer. "What's this?"

"Open it."

"Is this an engagement ring?"

"You won't believe this. Seriously, you will not believe what I'm about to tell you."

"Should I be sitting down for this? Are you getting engaged to her already?"

"No, no. Not at all. She was beautiful and smart and cute, but we were instantaneous friends. Nothing more. We ended up talking about Lydia and everything. By the end of it we were in front of a jewelry store. She made me realize my love for Lydia. She told me to buy a ring and when I propose it will be like falling in love all over again, like the newness I was looking for in someone else. Then I hesitated and what she said really struck me."

"Yes?"

"She said, 'Look, think of it like this. The old you is about to die and the new, better you is about to fall in love with the girl of your dreams. It wasn't the girl who needed to change, it was you all along. You were the one with the issues, not her. You were the one who needed to die, so that your relationship could live. No marriage can ever thrive without two people who are willing to die. Two selfish people make a miserable love story. One selfless person and one selfish person make an okay love story that may or may not continue depending on how selfless the one person is. But when two people are selfless . . . you will have the most beautiful love story in the world and it will only get better with time.'"

"Wow." Gavin's eyes lit up. "Well, I have a confession."

"What?"

"The letter you sent to Lydia. The one you gave me and I put in the mailbox. Remember?"

"Yes."

"I never gave it to her. I wanted you to think you had the closure you needed. And I intentionally set you up on horrible dates so that you would be forced to realize what a beautiful woman you already had. I didn't have anything to do with this last one, but I'm thankful she came into your life too. It was almost like you needed to meet her and hear those words from her to finally see the truth. Not sure I could ever put something quite as eloquently as she did."

"So Lydia never got the letter?" I sighed and sat down at the dining room table. "Oh, thank God."

"She never got it. And I also told her that you needed some time to think, but that I'd knock some sense into you. She's still waiting for you, Matt. She told me she'd wait forever if she needed to. She wanted you or nothing. Just like Heidi feels about Andy."

I bit my lower lip as I tried to hold back tears. "Wow. I don't deserve this, Gavin. I don't deserve her at all."

"No, you really don't. But it's time to change that. So, what's your plan for the big proposal?"

"You'll see."

"When are you doing it?"

"Are you kidding me? I can barely stand waiting right now. I'm doing it tomorrow."

I DIDN'T SLEEP AT ALL. I COULDN'T. WHEN THE FIRST PEEK OF daylight entered my room I shot up and got in the shower. It really did feel like falling in love all over again. The excitement of seeing her, hearing her voice again. I couldn't wait. Especially knowing what I was about to do.

After my shower I ran a few errands and picked up a few things for the proposal. By the time I got back Gavin had woken and showered too. Good timing.

"Hey," I said. "Can you help me now or is it too early?"

"It's early, but I'm ready. I'm excited for you too. A little jealous."

"Don't be jealous. Your time will come. I talked to Ella about her roommate Sarah, the one photographer you are teaching to paint."

"Are you serious? I told you I'm not into her like that."

"Well, anyway, she's taken. But you never know."

"Not like I'm looking around anyway. I'm fine being single. Just need to figure out what I'm going to do when you leave. How very depressed I will be."

"Yeah. It just won't be the same without my melancholy tunes."

"Alright, so what do you need me to do?"

"For starters, we need to get this piano to Neshaminy Creek."

"Nesaminy Creek? Why on earth?"

"Trust me. It will be worth it."

In silent anticipation, we moved the piano outside to the moving truck I rented, then lifted it up and placed it inside.

"What's all this?" Gavin pointed at the large bags in the back.

"I have a lot planned for this. I'm going to send her around a little scavenger hunt and at the end she'll come to Neshaminy Creek. It's a place that means a lot to us. I'm going to have the piano there and play her a song."

"Wow. I don't know if I'll be able to top this if I ever find a nice woman to call my own. So what's with all the bags of stuff?"

"A bazillion and one rose petals. More rose petals than I've ever seen in my life. It's going to be insane."

"Yes. Apparently." Gavin jumped out of the truck.

I shut the back door and unlocked the drivers side. "Can you come and help me set it up? Maybe wait for me until she gets close?"

"You saying I can't stick around and spy on the big moment?"

# Ch. 21 | Ella

My phone woke me up on Saturday morning. Along with a text from Matt: *Ella, thanks so much for your encouragement. I've got everything planned for tomorrow. I'll send you a pic when I get it all set up.*

I added his name to my phone. And tears poured down my cheeks. I couldn't help it if I tried. I wiped my face with my sheets and curled back up, staring at his text. His name in my phone. The name of dashed dreams and relentless fantasies turned nightmares.

I saw a new voicemail pop up and clicked the button to play it.

"Ella, it's me. Hey, we have someone who is buying the property from us. It should all be officially settled by the end of this month. They are going to turn it into a parking garage, so if you could have your things packed up as soon as possible that would be great. Leave anything you don't want and we'll take care of it. I'm so sorry about this, but there are probably plenty of places in Philly you could find to use. I hope it all works out. Call me if you have questions."

I rubbed my eyes and stared at my ceiling. "So, this is what it feels like when life crumbles to the ground."

Well, if I learned anything from Sarah's experience, I learned that it's okay to cry, but now it's time to get up, smile, and figure something out.

And that's just the thing. Today I vowed to not try to figure anything out about tomorrow. Today I decided to live today only.

Another tear warmed my cheeks. I covered my head and went back to sleep.

I WOKE TO MY PHONE BEEPING AT NOON. ANOTHER TEXT from Matt. *Check this out*, he said. Along with a picture of a beautiful scene. His piano by a river or lake, I couldn't tell. A million rose petals scattered all over the grass and piano. Pink and white and green. Surreal. Absolutely unbelievable on so many levels.

My phone beeped again. This time a text from Dee. *You coming in today? Didn't see you. Wanted to know how the date went. Was it him?*

I typed, *He is really nice and I'm pretty sure it was him. Yes. It was him. But he is about to propose to someone else. He's happy. It's where he is meant to be. I just don't know where I'm supposed to be anymore.*

A few minutes passed. I blinked, stared, blinked, cried, and repeated until Dee's text popped up. *I can't believe it was him. Are you okay?*

*Fine. It will take me a day to get over it, but I need to get up and live. This is the closure I needed. I think it's actually helping me to find life again. And Chances will be history next month. New owner turning it into a parking lot. We'll talk soon. I'll be in Monday to start packing up. Close up tonight and we'll put a closing up shop sign there. No more business after today.*

She called, but I didn't pick up. So she texted again. *Let me know if you need anything.*

*I'm fine. I promise. This is the start of my new life. I'm being forced to live again. It's good. I just need to cry it out first.*

And with that, I turned my phone off. A new beginning can't happen without the death of an old beginning. And so the hopes of my future died as I cried myself to sleep, giving up my dreams of tomorrow for something better. Life today.

# Ch. 22 | Matthew

Surrounded by thousands of pink and white rose petals, I waited at my piano underneath the willow tree. The branches hid the spot where we carved our initials when we first got together. Under the initials I painted, "Will you marry me, my sweetheart?" I tried to carve it, but it didn't show up well enough. Didn't want her to miss it.

I sent her on a scavenger hunt around the city. Every place she went to would be a meaningful place in the story of our relationship. I went to each place and put a small card with the next clue. Eventually, hopefully, she would make it to me.

My hands shook. My t-shirt clung to me with drops of sweat. Every now and then I'd laugh out loud, then play a song on the piano, pace around the petals, sit back down, and repeat. At least I played happy songs. Gavin would be proud.

A text from him showed up on my phone. *She just passed my car. Didn't see me. She should be there in 5. Let me know how it goes. So excited for you.*

I ran my fingers down the keys of the piano, remembering her smile as we sang this song together for the first time. It didn't make sense at the time. We just played a bunch of Lennon songs because she loves him and The Beatles. We happened upon this one and ended up kissing before we finished. Now, everything about the song made so much sense.

Hands on the keys, feet tapping the petals beneath me, eyes ahead, heart on my sleeve, I waited.

Behind the rustling of the willow tree I saw her hair lit by the sun, blowing out of her face as she walked toward me. I looked at the keys, back to her, back to the keys, and couldn't remember which song I wanted to play.

Everything blurred, like one of Gavin's paintings splashed by the rain. My hands remembered. I started to play, then sing along, "Our life together is so precious together. We have grown together, we have grown. Although our love is still special. Let's take a chance and fly away somewhere alone. . . ."

She walked closer. Smile stretching to California. Eyes on me. I played my heart out as she stood beside me, tears in her eyes, listening. My voice shook a few times, leading me to the end of the third verse. I sang it as best I could, "It'll be just like starting over, starting over." Then my voice cracked and I grabbed her hand, got on both knees in front of her, and kissed her hand over and over and over again.

"I'm sorry," I whispered, kissing her fingers, her wrist, her arm.

"Stand up," she said. "I'm sorry too, Matthew. I'm so sorry."

I looked up at her glistening eyes. "Sorry for what? You have nothing to be sorry for."

She squeezed my fingers and held my face with her other hand. "I'm sorry for walking out and leaving you like that."

"Sweetheart. Oh, you are too good for me."

I looked down and asked her to look at the tree.

She dropped to her knees in front of me. Forced me to look into her eyes. Face in her hands, I waited to hear the words that would start the next chapter of my life. My future with the most beautiful wife in the world.

She wrapped her arms around my neck and pressed her body into mine. We stayed like that for minutes, embracing and crying. I ran my fingers through her curled hair, straightening out the hours of work she put into them.

Smiling, I said, "So, what's your answer?"

"Oh, Matthew. You know my answer. My heart married you long before you ever put a ring on my finger."

"The ring!"

"What?"

"I forgot the ring." I shook my head. "How could I be so stupid?"

She laughed, wiping her cheeks. "You are the only for me."

"I can't believe I forgot the ring."

"I don't care about a ring, don't you see? I married you a long time ago. Rings, wedding cakes, they are nothing compared to the way it feels to be with you and to finally have you wake up and realize what we have."

We sat in the grass together, talking about our memories and our future life together. How many kids we would have, where we would live, what color bridesmaids dresses we would choose. Eventually we fell back into the petals and talked until the sun went down.

"We should go," she said, sitting up.

I pulled her back down and kissed her. "I want to marry you tomorrow. I don't want to wait."

"We waited this long. Let's do it right."

The sun said it's final goodbye for the day as we stood to leave. I couldn't bear the thought of waiting to marry her, but knew the sun would set for a few more months before I'd see her walking down the aisle to me. And like Ella said, I needed to die. To let my desires become whatever my Lydia wanted.

We walked to her car, swaying our locked hands back and forth.

One last kiss goodbye.

"This is home," I said. "You are home to me."

I now understood the feeling. As I watched her drive off, taillights rounding a corner and drifting out of sight, I understood the way Andy and Heidi must have felt the time she played the guitar for him. Home. In the arms of my woman. And as she drove away a part of my very self stretched across the road. For the first time in years I ached watching her leave. And I couldn't wait to wake up and see her tomorrow.

My future wife.

# Ch. 23 | Ella

Monday morning I unlocked the doors of *Chances* and thought of the irony. Really, what are the chances of finally meeting Mr. Right only to realize my entire purpose in his life was to ship him off to another woman? Only me.

Dee walked up as the front door closed.

I opened it and smiled. "Ready to shut this place down?"

"Not really," she said. "We have a lot of catching up to do first."

"I really don't want to talk about Matt. Really, truly, don't want to talk about him."

We walked behind the counter and Dee turned on one of the espresso machines. "I"m making us some coffee, we're pulling up a chair over there, and we're talking. There's no way I'm letting you hold all this inside. Have you talked to Sarah?"

"I haven't. Not yet. She's been so busy lately. Her and her boyfriend, who I have yet to meet, are with each other all the time. I don't understand if she's so serious about him why she doesn't introduce him to me. It all seems so secretive and bizarre."

"Maybe she's not as into him as you think."

I shrugged, looked around at the art on the walls, the books on the shelves in the corner, the cute tables and chairs I picked out, the sign on the door. "I had so much hope when I started this place."

"You don't have hope anymore?"

"I do. It's just different. My hope is to truly live one day at a time. To enjoy life regardless of whether I'm single or married. The hope of him died."

"Yes, but I guess this is the closure you needed to move on with your life."

I lifted my body on to the counter and pulled my feet up. "Closure. Yes. This chapter has finally ended, but it wasn't the ending I was hoping for."

"Well, like I said before, sometimes you have to stop being so idealistic and realize that love doesn't always end up like the movies."

"It doesn't always, but it does sometimes. Tylissa and Mwenye have a beautiful movie-like romance. And the most beautiful thing is that it gets more beautiful every day. They are the most devoted people I've ever met. Devoted to love, to each other, to others."

"Let me help you keep things in perspective here. The guy you spotted across the coffee shop years ago. He is getting married to someone else. It was a strange and odd dream you had. To really believe you would find this guy and fall in love. It could happen, I guess, but what are the chances? I know, I know, that's why you named this place *Chances*. That's why you stopped taking chances and lived within these walls waiting for him. But the reality is he is in love with someone else. It doesn't end there, though. The other piece of this reality is that you are free to fall in love with someone else now, and there's no reason you can't walk out this door right now, trip over the curb, and land in Prince Charming's arms."

I laughed. "Wow. What a speech. The ending is definitely Ella-esque."

"There's always Patrick."

"No, no, no. Absolutely not Patrick."

"He is so charming. And depressed. And lonely. Cheer him up and live happily ever after."

"That's, um, quite the romance if you ask me." I hopped off the counter and took the coffee she handed me. "It's not Patrick. No idea who, if anyone, the man for me will be. But I have to say I kind of like the mystery in this."

My phone beeped. When would his name stop making me feel like I lost a part of myself?

"Who's that? You look like you saw an apparition float out of your phone."

I showed her the screen.

"Wow," she said. "That has to be the most over the top proposal I have ever seen in my life."

"Yes. He played one of her favorite songs for her with all those petals around."

The phone beeped and she handed it to me.

I turned my phone off and sighed. "He wants to invite me to their wedding."

"Sounds delightful." She sipped her coffee and looked around the room. "So what do we do first? Take down the pictures? What are you taking? And what are you going to do next?"

I stood in front of the painting of Matt and Lydia. "Well, I'll start here. Keep these as we take them down. I want to give them back to the artists."

"Okay." Dee started at the other end of the shop. "So, what are you doing next?"

"You know what, Dee? I have no idea. I'm letting this place go. Letting my past go. And I'm just going to wake up tomorrow and see what the day has for me."

"That sounds nice, but you need another job."

"I know. I am considering moving away from Philly, using the money I've saved to start another company. Not sure what. Something different. Something opposite of running a coffee shop."

"Understandable."

Together we lifted all of the art work off the walls until we reached each other. The bare walls spoke of a newness I couldn't describe. Thoughts warred against each other in my mind though. Constant tug-of-war between excitement and sadness. I spent the last decade standing in front of a door, admiring the beauty of what I believed I'd see if I walked inside. Finally my moment came. The door creaked and a slight breeze blew it open. The inside didn't look as beautiful as I imagined, but before I could really see inside the door slammed in my face. Locked. Never to be opened again.

There's an excitement when you walk away from such doors. You know they're closed forever and you walk away looking up again. You spent so long staring at the door, wondering what lived inside, that you forgot about the trees, the clouds, the sunlight casting shadows on the earth. And a new excitement birthed inside of me. An excitement as I walked from the door and saw the beauty I missed for so long.

But with that came a heaviness. A deep ache. Lost in a swirling mix of emotions, I knew the truth as much as I didn't want to. Dreams die, yes, I saw that now. But it took all I had to not allow hope to die along with them.

DEE AND I SPENT THE ENTIRE DAY CLOSING DOWN THE SHOP. A few people knocked on the door, asked what happened. We explained and they went on their merry way. Seconds after we flipped the light switch to call it a night we heard another knock at the window. A sleek woman and a cameraman stood outside, waving, smiling.

"Oh, great," I said, not budging.

Dee opened the door. "Can I help you with something?"

"Yes, we'd like to interview Ella about the shop and what she plans to do next."

I inched toward the door. "Why not broadcast the losing hand to the entire casino?"

Dee laughed. "Go for it."

I walked outside and introduced myself.

"This is going to be live," she said. "So try to speak quick and to the point. We don't have much time."

"Remind me why this is interesting enough for the news?" I said as she flipped my hair in front of my shoulder.

"Anything is. It's a story. Stories are always interesting."

I'll give her something really interesting, I thought. "Here's to you, Patrick."

"Ready?" she said, cuing the camera guy and holding the speaker in her ear.

# Ch. 24 | Matthew

Lydia wanted to spend the next few days enjoying each other and not rushing into wedding plans, but I couldn't help it. We sat on my couch, her body tucked under my arm and her legs wrapped around my legs.

"Let's get married in the spring. It's only a few months from now. Gives us enough time to plan."

"Okay." She waved her finger at me. "But nothing extravagant. I don't want a ton of people and a big party. This is our love we're celebrating and only people who have been supportive and part of our story should be there."

"I agree. A small, intimate wedding sounds better anyway. I don't want to walk away feeling exhausted that night."

Gavin walked in the door, suit and tie and everything. "Look at you two love birdies, chirping away."

"Hey, Gavin," Lydia said.

"How was your day?" I chimed in. "Did you get the job for the theatre?"

"Don't know yet." He slumped into the couch across from us, loosened his tie, and flicked on the television. "Long day. Wondering with you two lovebirds leaving the nest soon if I should find a new tree to live in."

"Where would you go?" Lydia said.

"No idea. I guess I'd be like Gump. Just start running."

"That would be interesting." I said, then noticed a familiar face on the television screen. "Hey, look. It's Ella from *Chances*."

"We're here tonight with Ella Rhodes from *Chances*. This is her last night at the cafe. And not too long ago it was her first. This entire block will soon be bought out and turned into yet another parking garage. Ella, do you plan on relocating?"

"I don't have any plans."

"What made you start this place? Is it sad to see it turned into a parking garage so soon?"

"A little. Years ago I came to this cafe as a customer. I sat down by the window right here." She pointed behind her. "And I saw a young man at the time who caught my eye and had kept my heart since. I fell in love with him without ever speaking to him. When I started *Chances* I did so in hopes of seeing him walk in the door one day and into my life."

"Did he?"

"Yes."

"And what happened?"

"He walked back out. I escorted him to the door and back to the woman he's meant to be with, which isn't me. We were set up on a blind date after he became a familiar customer here and after seeing how much he loved this girl and didn't remember me, I had to let him go. Just like I have to let *Chances* go, too."

I looked at Gavin. Lydia looked at me. Standing up, I covered my mouth with my hands. I knew Ella looked familiar. My heart flopped around my chest like a fish out of water.

"Lydia," I said. "It's not what you think."

I looked at Gavin. His eyes were glued to the screen. Glued to the story unfolding in front of us. We waited the last ten years to turn the page.

The news segment ended. Ella's face disappeared. Replaced by two make-upped faces sitting at a desk, mesmerized with the story Ella told. The story that seemed too unreal to be real.

But it was real.

"Gavin?"

Eyes still on the screen, he wiped a single tear from his cheek.

"I've been waiting ten years for this moment," he said, then ran right out the front door.

I looked at Lydia. "We have to follow him. Ella is the girl he's been waiting for. They saw each other across the coffee shop years ago. I mean, years ago. He hasn't talked about her much. Didn't want to get his hopes up. That's definitely her. And the fact that she started *Chances* just to see him again. I can't believe this."

"Let's go." Lydia stood. "I can't miss this. I think I'm going to cry, too."

We made our way out of the apartment building and to the busy city street. The evening sun painted the buildings gold. A perfect night.

We jogged to catch up to Gavin, but didn't see him. Finally, out of breath, Lydia and I stopped in front of *Chances*. I tugged the door. Nothing. Lights out. A cafe once filled with the aroma of coffee and signs of life, now vacant.

"There he is," Lydia said, pointing across the street.

Leaned up against a building, Gavin shook his head at us. We waited for cars to clear and crossed the street.

"Hey, don't look so down," I said. "You forgot she still has your artwork and probably plans to return it to you."

"How? She doesn't have my address."

"Good point."

Lydia tapped my shoulder. "Can't you call Dee? Or Sarah?"

Gavin grabbed Lydia's arms and kissed her cheek. "Brilliant. Why didn't we think of that?"

"I really have no idea." She smiled and linked her fingers with mine. "Silly men."

Gavin searched his phone for Sarah's number and called five times in a row. No answer. I tried Dee. Five times. No answer.

"Wait a second. I have Ella's number." I looked at Gavin's bright face. "But she thinks I'm you. No wonder she hasn't responded to my texts since we met."

"Give me your phone," he said. "I want to call her myself."

I handed it to him, but Lydia swiped it. "That is not the way you want to go about this. Trust me. We have her number. We can get in touch with her. Let's make this more romantic than an awkward phone call."

"Good idea," I said. "Just as long as it doesn't beat my proposal."

"It's a good idea, but I can't wait that long. I've waited years for this. Kept everything bottled inside like a shaken soda can about to pop. It's killing me. I have to see her right now."

Lydia gave the phone to Gavin. We looked at each other as he dialed the number. The setting sun reflected in her eyes.

I kissed her eyelids. "I love you, Lydia Rae."

"I love you too, Matthew."

She snuggled into my chest as I ran my fingers down her arm and stopped at her hand.

Gavin gave me the phone. "Her phone is turned off."

"Now what?" I said.

"I have to find her. Keep your phone on. I'm going this way. Seriously, I'm going to search this city until I find her. If you see her, call me right away. Don't tell her about me though. I want to be the one to say it. Just keep her there until I come."

"And if you find her?"

"I'll be back from Vegas by Thursday. Don't wait up for me."

Lydia laughed. "I hope you're not serious."

Gavin jogged out of sight. I've never seen such joy in his face as I did that night.

"We have to find her first," Lydia said.

"Why?"

"Because I have to see this. It's too good to be true."

I touched her cheek and pushed her hair behind her ear, then leaned in and whispered, "This is too good to be true, too."

She never stopped smiling as we walked Philadelphia streets until our feet practically fell off our ankles. The sun set on us as it rose on another love story. The streets, now lit artificially, guided us back to my apartment.

I pulled the front door open for Lydia and the phone rang. We stopped. My hand fell from the door and reached in my pocket.

"Hey, Dee," I said. "You'll never believe this."

"This better be good. You called five times in a row."

"It is good. Very good. Listen, do you know about the guy Ella created *Chances* for?"

"Yes. I believe you may not remember, but it just so hap—"

"No, Dee. It's not me. It's Gavin."

"But she said she remembered your shoes. The Converse ones."

I laughed. "Of course. And that may be true, because the night Gavin saw her in the cafe I happened to be standing right beside him."

"What kind of weirdo wears the same shoes for ten years?"

"A boring story for a rainy day. Right now, we need to find Ella. Gavin is searching Philadelphia for her as we speak."

"Wow. This is amazing. Okay, well, here's the problem. We just went out to eat and I think she's probably already at her apartment by now. She said she wanted to walk home to get her car and drive to the beach to watch the sunrise. Something she used to do in her past and hasn't done in a while. She's trying to live a little, I guess. Her heart is broken. She thinks it was you."

"I know. Alright, when does she plan to come back?"

"Tomorrow, I guess."

"Where does she live? Can you give me her address?"

"I'm not sure. It's that really pretty building. Almost looks like a hotel. It's not far from the shop."

"Are you kidding me?"

"What?"

"All this time she has practically lived right next door to us. I bet she could hear my piano when I left the window open."

I hung up with Dee and called Gavin immediately, told him what happened, and asked him to please try to get some sleep tonight.

"Definitely ain't gonna happen."

"Are you going to drive to the beach?"

"Maybe."

"You're probably running full speed back here to get your car, aren't you?"

"About to."

He hung up and I put my phone back in my pocket. Lydia and I said our goodbye's. I begged her to stay longer, but she had to work early.

# Ch. 25 | Ella

I finished my interview, closed up the shop, and Dee and I walked to a restaurant to meet up with Sarah for dinner. We talked about nothing important, per my request. I had enough people asking questions already. I knew I'd get a call from someone in my family asking me why I had to be so rash and close down the shop before the settlement was confirmed. Hence the turned off phone. I wanted to move on. Just be done. And that's all there is to it.

Dee, Sarah, and I parted ways after dinner. Sarah decided to drive to her boyfriend's house. Mystery man. Dee walked to her apartment in the opposite direction. So thankful for all of her help. We packed the entire shop up in one day. Everything I wanted to keep fit in my car, along with the paintings I needed to try to return.

I decided to walk home, get in my car, and drive to the Jersey shore. Alone. Like old times.

On my way back home I passed *Chances*. Emptied. I stopped and pressed my face against the glass where it said *Chances* in white script.

The violin someone purchased for me sat in a box by the counter. I forgot it.

I pulled out my key one last time and opened the door, walked inside, and sat on a chair in the middle of the room. Bare walls. Kind of like my life. Anything goes now, I thought. Where will life take me?

I walked to the counter and picked up a piece of paper, wrote something, and taped it to the window with packing tape.

*Sometimes when you take chances you lose chances. And sometimes when you lose chances, you gain something else. Don't live for chances. Sometimes it's better to lose chances and gain purpose. Live for today. You'll find so much more joy.*

Kind of a note to myself to be honest. But I figured so many people saw me on the news and it couldn't hurt to inspire them a little. I wasn't as depressed as I probably came across on television.

Or was I?

I turned back to the violin case, picked it up and took the instrument out, then ran my fingers along the strings and stopped at the neck. Some strange fear still lived inside of me. Fear of failure. Fear of chasing dreams after killing the life of another person. A little boy. Fear of placing the violin on my shoulder, running the bow across the strings, and not being able to play a single note like I could before.

I sat down facing the counter, put the violin to my shoulder, and waited.

The clock on the wall haunted me with its rhythm, begging me to add a melody. A melody from the past.

"Okay, clock," I said. "I will play something for you, but not a melody from the past. A melody from the future. And yes, I'm going to be hopeful. Bear with me here."

I picked up the bow and straightened my shoulders. I started soft and low, shaky, then found myself in the midst of the beautiful, soft sound of Pachelbel's *Canon in D*. Back and forth, back and forth. I closed my eyes. Let my fears go. Saw Parker's face and tried to imagine him running around in the grass, blowing bubbles and popping them as they fell. I played with more passion that I think I ever did. The song swelled. Echoing and bouncing off the walls. Filling me with something I hadn't felt in so long.

Something I couldn't even describe.

The song picked up pace. I loved this part. So beautiful. I imagined myself walking down the aisle. To someone else. Someone even better. White dress trailing behind me. Veil covering my face. A tall, dark-haired man smiling at the altar. Waiting for me. For us. For our life together.

Someone knocked on the window.

I stopped. Turned. Violin still in my hands, I saw a man outside holding a small piece of paper against the window, covering his face. A little scared, I walked toward him with the bow and instrument dangling at my sides. Not sure who looked crazier, him or me.

I could barely read the small letters on the note. I squinted.

*The best things come to those who wait.*

Confused, I peeked around the note to his face.

His face. His eyes. His smile. The same smile. The same eyes. The same face. From all those years ago.

I dropped the violin and the bow. I tried so hard not to cry. He looked at me. I looked at him. Frozen on the other side of the glass, one tear started down my face and turned into a stream.

Tears landing in his smile, he laughed. So did I.

I put my hand on the window while I covered my mouth with the other. He touched his fingertips to mine, then ran toward the door and into the shop. Into my life.

We embraced. His warm arms tight around my body. My face pressed into his chest. No words were needed. We stepped back. His eyes on me. My eyes on him. We said, "Hi," over and over again, held on for dear life, and repeated, until he pulled away and held my hands.

We stared at each other, through each other, like we had been together in this moment for years. He touched my cheek, then my lips. I closed my eyes as his face inched toward mine. Soft and sweet, we kissed as ink began to cover the bare walls of my life. The story continued. Better than I could've imagined.

I opened my eyes. Looked into his. Smiles lighting up the room, he finally broke the silence by clearing his throat. I realized I hadn't heard his voice before. I didn't know his name. And all that would change. Right now.

He smiled and shook his head. "What are the chances?"

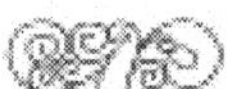

Gavin Kessler's one of the most sensitive and emotional people you'd ever know, except you'd never know it. Trying to find out how he feels is like pulling a one-hundred pound bucket of water out of a seventy foot well. But when he finally falls in love and meets the woman of his dreams, who is set on getting to know every part of him, for better or worse, his walls crumble as he is forced to stand face-to-face with the past he's been avoiding.

Continue to follow the stories of your favorite characters from *Where Love Finds You* in this sequel, *Down from the Clouds*, written from Gavin's perspective.

**COMING WINTER 2014**

Made in the USA
Lexington, KY
20 December 2015